TROUBLE & THE WALLFLOWER

Kade Boehme

Dreamspinner Press

Published by
Dreamspinner Press
5032 Capital Circle SW
Suite 2, PMB# 279
Tallahassee, FL 32305-7886
USA
http://www.dreamspinnerpress.com/

Trouble & the Wallflower
© 2014 Kade Boehme.

Cover Art
© 2014 Leah Kaye Suttle.
www.leahsuttle.com.
Cover content is for illustrative purposes only and any person depicted on the cover is a model.

ISBN: 978-1-62798-448-5
Digital ISBN: 978-1-62798-447-8

Printed in the United States of America
First Edition
February 2014

ACKNOWLEDGMENTS

Thanks to Wendy for reminding me to take a break and keeping me sane. Ang, for making me laugh when I need it most. Sey, Ames, and Taylor, you all make my life brighter.

And to Mon. Thanks for planting the tiniest of ideas that turned into these boys I'll never forget.

CHAPTER ONE

DAVY PASSED a cone loaded with two black-licorice ice cream scoops to a beaming toddler who bounced in her father's arms. After a thanks and a tip from the dad, Davy gave his typical shy smile-and-nod routine. He was pretty sure he was the only person who ever managed to get tips off shyness, but he figured that working in an old-fashioned soda shop where the majority of clientele were tourists and children, being unassuming was preferable to being overeager. People were at ease around his shy nature, and it paid his bills.

The bell that hung above the door jingled, followed by laughter, signaling that he had customers. As he turned to greet them, he couldn't even muster a smile when he recognized the group of five guys walking in. Okay. So there was occasionally something about his job that wasn't quite so comfortable, and these guys—more specifically one of these guys—rattled his cage, and he wasn't sure why.

Well, that was a lie. He knew why. They were around his age and attractive, his opposites in every way, and they were guys. Cute guys. They had the hipstery look of most Seattle twentysomethings and spoke freely with one another, laughing raucously at their own ridiculousness. They came in at least once a week. In fact, he knew most of their orders by heart at this point. He also knew they were all openly gay after having heard plenty of their carefree conversations. He knew they were students, and all of them worked in the area surrounding the market at Pike's Place.

He'd seen most of them daily, though he was certain they never noticed him. Not many people did. He liked it that way. But one of them always noticed him. Whether they were in Bart's Soda Shop where Davy worked or if they bumped into each other on the street, this one guy rattled him the most because he saw Davy.

Davy had figured out the guy's name was Gavin, mostly because the guy had told him. About a hundred times. Gavin always zeroed right in on Davy, even as the rest of the world passed quiet Davy by as if he were a ghost. It was unnerving. Davy didn't know what to do around other guys in general. He could sit in the club for hours being a wallflower, seeing the occasional guy look his way, and never once leave his spot. He'd flee before anyone thought to approach him. He wasn't a total freak, but being around other guys, especially gay men, tended to make him a nervous wreck. But damn if he never gave up.

Gavin, with his beanies and skinny jeans that hung low in the crotch and his wicked grin that sported two devastating dimples, was definitely someone Davy couldn't ignore. And those eyes. Big brown eyes shadowed by his ridged forehead and prominent eyebrows. Those eyebrows were perfect. Dimples and glinting brown eyes aside, Davy had heard enough of their conversations to know Gavin wasn't exactly a blushing virgin. Not by a long shot. Davy didn't intend to be a notch on that guy's bedpost any time soon. Not that he was a notch on many guys' bedposts willingly, but he did his damnedest to avoid it where this guy was concerned.

Of course, Gavin's gaze locked on Davy's before anyone else's as his small group of friends made it to the counter. Gavin shot Davy what he must have thought was his most winning grin. Davy gave his usual response—he rolled his eyes. Gavin laughed, his friends shook their heads at him, but he was never discouraged, damn him. He hung back as usual as his friends came up one at a time to order their milkshakes, floats, and cones. Davy kept peeking out of the corner of his eye as, one by one, he handed each of the other guys their treats. They looked at him apologetically, rolling their eyes right along with him, always confirming that the only reason they came in the shop was so Gavin could throw himself at his potential conquest.

Davy often wondered how Gavin was so certain Davy was gay. But it still seemed he was way too quiet for anyone to make an assumption other than perhaps thinking he was asexual. Perhaps Gavin hit on all men that shamelessly, but he seemed overly confident that he might have a chance with Davy. Which he did not. At all.

Finally it was Gavin's turn, and Davy plastered on his best fake smile but crossed his arms over his chest as Gavin slid smoothly up to the counter, with that annoyingly sexy smile and those devilish eyes, and leaned in as close as he could, elbows propped on the top of the counter, chin in his hands. Davy quirked an eyebrow as Gavin shamelessly appraised him, causing Davy to blush. Damn how easily he blushed for giving him away every time. Didn't matter that his skin was naturally a honeyed tan, his blush still shone bright on his high cheekbones. Gavin's smile grew smug every time Davy's cheeks colored, and it really pissed Davy off. Another one of many reasons he wouldn't give this guy the time of day.

"Heya, Davy."

Gavin's voice dripped with suggestion and Davy rolled his eyes. Again.

"Hello, sir. Cherry limeade, as usual?" Davy kept his tone even.

Gavin gripped his heart dramatically, and his friends snickered behind him. Davy pursed his lips in annoyance. "Ouch, Dave-o. I remember your name. Do I mean so little to you?"

"Less than you'd think," Davy said with a glare. He hated this guy for getting a rise out of him. He tried to tell himself it was because he couldn't stand the guy, but he knew it was because he actually wanted to jump the counter and lick the guy from head to toe. Thankfully Gavin didn't know he was the only person who inspired any type of reaction out of Davy, who was normally shy enough he wouldn't back-talk someone who jumped in front of him in line. Damn this Gavin dude.

Gavin leaned in again with a smirk. "Now, I just don't think that's so, Davy. I don't see you talking smack to my friends. I don't see you talk back to anyone, really. So I think you're just playing hard to get."

Shit. "Whatever." *Clever.*

Gavin's eyes practically widened in excitement. Davy's lack of a poker face must have shown Gavin he was right. Although he'd call it "never gonna get" before he'd say "hard to get." He looked to Gavin's friends, beseeching the strangers with his eyes to intervene. They were all too busy turning red from laughter or shrugging apologetically. No help there. Before he embarrassed himself with this jackass any further, Davy turned to the soda station and started squeezing limes for the cherry limeade. He just wanted them gone.

He concentrated on the work at hand, breathing in and out. If only Gavin understood. He'd give anything to be normal enough to just take his number one of the million times he'd offered it. He'd love to go have that coffee with him. But Davy wasn't normal. He was struggling past a panic attack now. The only thing stopping him from freaking out totally was the familiar actions. Cut the lime in half, juice it, add sugar and carbonated water. Shake. Shit. He forgot grenadine. He had to look at Gavin again because the grenadine was under the counter. Damn. He avoided eye contact, but he could feel the smirk on Gavin's face, and part of him wanted to throw the guy's drink in his face. The rest of him wanted to run into the back and hide. He hated being noticed. Why couldn't Gavin just figure that out?

When he went to pour the drink into a to-go cup, Gavin cleared his throat, making Davy look up at him, startled. "Something got you flustered?"

Gavin's smugness really, *really* made Davy reconsider running and vote for slinging the drink in the guy's cocky mug. Gavin nodded down at Davy's hands, and Davy noticed he'd dumped the damn limeade on the floor instead of into the cup.

Shit!

Davy had to control the growl that wanted to escape.

Get a grip. Now Gavin's friends were in full hysterics, and Davy hated them for it. He wanted to die. He flung the cup in the trash, turned to make another limeade, and poured it into the cup this time instead of on the floor. "On the house," he said. *Please just leave.*

Gavin held his hands out as if he was surrendering.

"No, no, no. I insist." Gavin pulled some cash out of the pocket on his plaid button-down shirt.

4

"I messed up the first one, so this one's on the house." Davy flashed his best grin at the friends, then with a "Have a good afternoon," he escaped into the back room, wishing he could get farther away from Gavin than that. From the stockroom he could hear choruses of "shameless" and "creeper" from Gavin's cackling crew of friends.

After the bell over the door signaled their departure, Davy waited for their laughter to recede, like the coward he was, then sighed and headed back out into the shop. He came up short as soon as he opened the curtain that separated the front counter and the back rooms. Gavin was still there, leaning on the counter and sucking on his drink through a straw. Yeah, those lips wrapped around that straw held a promise. A promise Davy had to will his body to ignore. All he needed was for that pest to see him get hard for him. This was one of those moments where Davy was sorry the employees had gotten rid of their uniform aprons, though he'd originally been the one to suggest it.

Gavin noticed Davy before he could even think of slipping back into the storeroom again, but he knew he'd look silly sneaking off.

"You didn't think I'd leave without giving you a tip, did you?"

There was that suggestive tone again. Who was this guy, The Most Interesting Man in the World? It was as though his voice dropped an octave just to sound sexy. It was as though he studied too many noir films to get his come-ons. Davy almost laughed at the idea of the shaggy-haired guy before him in a trench coat and fedora. Then Gavin's eyes got that predatory gleam again. *Shit.* He must have seen that almost-smile. *Shit.*

"Uh. Really, it wasn't necessary. I messed up." Davy busied himself with a mop, cleaning the spilled drink from the floor, but Gavin didn't take his hint to bugger off. But why should this time be any different?

"No. I insist." He made sure Davy saw him slip a ten-dollar bill in the tip jar.

Davy wanted to pull it out and throw it at him, but he couldn't turn down a tip. And didn't this guy know a tip was a tacky way to try to pick someone up? *What am I, a hooker?*

"You know, my gramps loves peanut-butter shakes. I remember you saying to someone that you made the best. Mind whipping one up for him? To go, of course."

Davy huffed. Damn was he glad his boss wasn't here to see him being so rude to a customer, but wasn't this sexual harassment, anyway? He had a sudden urge to look up how he could deal with that in the handbook. He hoped it involved pruning shears.

With a scowl, Davy scooped the ice cream and peanut butter to make the shake. He knew Gavin watched him the whole time and could feel his ears burning. Of course Gavin looked pleased with himself when Davy handed him the shake red-faced and fidgeting.

He laid down more cash on the counter. "Keep the change."

Davy looked at him defiantly. "That's ridiculous, Gavin."

"See! I knew you remembered!"

Gavin looked as though he'd won a prize. Damn him for being adorable when he was excited. And smug. Who made smug look cute? *Apparently Gavin.* Davy blamed it on that button nose and the dimples. Bastard. Gavin picked up one of the to-go menus they kept on the counter and a pen from beside the cash register, then jotted down his phone number for the millionth time. When he slid it across the counter toward Davy, they locked gazes, and Davy had to force himself to look away. Gavin chuckled. "Use it."

"Have a good afternoon," Davy said, using his most annoyed tone, which just got another chuckle from Gavin. *Oh yeah. Gavin's figured that trick out already.*

"See you next time, Davy."

Gavin's voiced dripped sex. Davy refused to look at him, wiping the counter viciously though there wasn't a smudge on it. The bastard had the nerve to chuckle all the way out of the store. When the door closed behind Gavin, Davy let out an exasperated grunt and smacked his hand on the counter. At least he had avoided a panic attack. He looked over at the to-go menu with the phone number and *Gavin Walker* written on it. Davy was always surprised at how neat Gavin's penmanship was. That didn't stop him from wadding up the paper and throwing it in the trash before removing the liner to take it to the dumpster.

Chapter Two

"Are you sure you don't need anything? I'll be in town next week. I can bring groceries." Davy's Uncle Drew meant well, but every time they talked on the phone, it ended like this. Davy stretched out on his couch, knowing this conversation wasn't ending anytime soon.

"Really, I'm cool. I promise." It was his automatic response. He knew his uncle was just worried about him, but he was being honest when he said it. His uncle was worried he was following in his mother's footsteps. Drew had helplessly watched his older sister's downward spiral into being a housebound agoraphobic. He checked on Davy daily, making sure he ventured out into the world. Davy definitely didn't consider himself that bad. Yeah, he had some social anxiety issues and was painfully shy, but unlike his mother, he would go stark raving mad if he stayed locked indoors all the time.

"If you're sure."

Drew sounded skeptical. He, like Gavin and his friends, was the opposite of Davy in almost every way. He was an attractive, outgoing gay man who took time out of his busy social schedule every afternoon to be a mother hen to his awkwardly shy nephew. Being an educator, he'd always been annoyed with Davy's mother's choice to homeschool her son. He was right, honestly, because even Davy knew his biggest issue was that he had absolutely no socialization other than work. He'd not spoken to anyone other than his elderly neighbors until he got the job at the soda shop when he was sixteen. His mother had been dead set against him leaving the house, but his uncle had talked her into it, and Davy found his first bit of freedom. It hadn't served him too well. His first fumblings with friends and boys were all unsuccessful because he was too naïve to realize when he was being played. He was wary of people, but certainly not of the sunshine and the busy streets of the city.

"Are you okay for money? I know you can't make enough to live on at that ice cream place." Drew was like a dog with a bone, but it made Davy smile while feeling warmth from the knowledge that he was lucky to have someone who cared.

"I've still got enough from financial aid and Mom's life insurance to make up the difference."

Drew harrumphed inelegantly. "Well, how are your online classes going?"

"They're good, Uncle Drew. I'm almost done, actually. I'll be able to get a big-boy job." *And Gavin won't be able to stalk me there.*

"That's great, Davy. If you need any help with your résumé...."

"I'll call you." Davy laughed. "I really should go finish some schoolwork, though."

"Davy, it's a Saturday! Fuck your homework! Go out. Have some fun."

Davy shook his head at his uncle's enthusiasm. He didn't know what the point of going out would be. He'd just sit in the background and watch other people have fun. His uncle wouldn't know what that was like. He was only twelve years older than Davy's twenty-two years, but he acted more Davy's age than Davy did. When he wasn't busy playing mommy/uncle, that was.

"I'll think about it," Davy said. He knew that was the only answer that would get his uncle off the phone.

Drew sighed in exasperation. "I know that's a no, but I'll leave you alone. Love you, man. Have a good night. If you need me, call Allie's phone. She's DD. She'll answer and get me."

"Night, Uncle Drew." Davy didn't give his uncle a chance to start rambling again and pressed the End Call button on his phone's touch screen. He tossed his phone down on his coffee table and rubbed his hands over his face. He sat up and looked around his spartan one-bedroom apartment. When he'd transferred to the smaller apartment after his mom's death a year earlier, he'd sold off most of her oversize furniture. He needed the money, and her stuff was way too ornate and feminine for him. Anything special went into a cheap storage unit down in Tukwila. His apartment was all bare walls and IKEA furniture. It was all he needed. Not like he entertained enough to need anything fancy. He was a loner and this was his space. He was cool with that.

You sure about that? his brain always teased him. He pictured plump lips and wicked brown eyes for a moment, and he definitely wasn't sure he was quite as happy being a loner as he once had been. Without his mom rattling around, his lack of human contact—a simple hug or a ruffle of his hair while he worked on his schoolwork—was starting to make his inner cuddle-bear desperate. Dammit.

He stood in a huff, pushing that thought away, and went to his fridge to stare inside for a minute. He wasn't hungry. Maybe he could go for a run. He shut the fridge and started pacing. He could always go biking. *Or you could listen to Drew and just go out.* No way. That wasn't an option.

Shut up, you. Stop being a baby.

Fuck it. He steeled his resolve. It was already ten. People would be out and about. One drink wouldn't hurt.

I KNEW this was a bad idea.

Davy sat in a booth, barely able to hear that thought for the *thumpa-thumpa* of the bassline of the song that had everyone else in the club grinding on one another. He sipped his second vodka and cranberry, wishing it'd give him the same courage it seemed to give other people to go out and mingle with the sexy guys having fun on the floor with their friends. Maybe even make out with someone. That'd be real nice. So far he'd only been approached by a go-go boy who'd sensed a lonely heart needing some entertainment, but the guy had given up when Davy couldn't even meet his gaze. Davy felt sufficiently lame and was beginning to think he should make his exit after he finished this drink. At least he'd gotten a nice buzz. That was about all he ever got out of a trip to the gay club. He was too busy hiding in the background. He also saw enough shirtless guys making out with each other to provide him with enough jerk-off material until his next visit.

He stood and shook his head at himself, then made his way to the bar to hand off his empty glass. The bartender asked if he needed another. Before he could finish saying no, a familiar group of guys walked up the stairs, drinks in hand and laughing. Gavin's buddies from the ice cream shop were all dressed to kill. And there was Gavin following behind them. He had a genuine smile. It almost took Davy's breath away. Gavin looked boyish and innocent when his grin wasn't that predatory Grinch grin Davy usually saw.

He was also a total stunner in his club clothes. A black wifebeater showed off sinewy muscles and smooth skin. He had several randomly placed tattoos that Davy's brain imagined licking. Twice. Gavin's bright-blue shorts showed off the man's sexy legs. *Sexy legs? Really? How drunk are you?*

The bartender tapped Davy's shoulder, and Davy jumped. The bartender had his eyebrows raised and impatiently repeated the question. Davy got a glimpse of Gavin taking one of his friend's hands and leading him out to the floor, where he started a sexy bump-and-grind. Davy's cheeks flushed at the thoughts the sensual movements of Gavin's trim hips inspired. He turned to the bartender and nodded. The bartender had obviously seen where Davy had been staring like a fool. Davy felt like an idiot for being so obvious, but the bartender smiled at him sympathetically and started making his drink. When he passed the vodka and cranberry over, Davy held out some cash. The guy held his hand up and shook his head. When Davy looked at him in confusion, the guy crooked his finger so Davy leaned in. The guy met him halfway and spoke loud enough to be heard over the music but not enough to be heard by anyone but Davy. "That guy, he's trouble."

"So why am I not paying for my drink?" Davy was so confused. Maybe it was the booze?

"Honey, if that's your type, the only way you'll stop hugging that wall is if you get some more of those in your system. That one's on me." Davy's face heated, and the bartender laughed. "Go and have fun, little wallflower. Just don't waste your time on idiots like that." Davy tried to thank the guy, but he was so embarrassed the words stuck in his throat, so he just nodded and went back to his booth. *One more drink. That's all*, he told himself. He just couldn't stop watching Gavin. He needed five more minutes to see the man in action. He knew it was lame—and creepy. But this Gavin, the one so sure of himself that he was sex on legs, who danced like that and owned that dance floor, was the Gavin who kept pulling Davy in. He wished he'd see more of this Gavin than that smug asshole Gavin turned into when he was in the shop.

Davy was halfway finished with his drink, and the DJ had put on a party-anthem song that had Gavin and his friends fist-pumping and bouncing around like idiots. Davy couldn't bring himself to be annoyed by it, because they were just having fun. There was nothing pretentious about them. They were just being the kind of guys Davy wished he could be. But there weren't enough vodka-cranberries in the world. His drink almost gone, he considered having just one more, but he noticed one of the go-go boys had made his way to Gavin. The go-go boy had a million-dollar smile, tight abs, and a thick ass. Davy totally didn't blame Gavin when he started dry-humping the guy in front of everyone. He guessed he didn't really blame him for playing tonsil hockey with him, either. But it made Davy's buzz fly right out the window.

He felt like a dumbass. This just confirmed why Gavin was a bad bet anyway. He went back over to the bar and handed the bartender his empty glass. The bartender gave him a sympathetic pat on the hand with an expression that looked a lot like *I told you so*. Fucker. "Thanks for the drink." Davy knew it didn't even register over the music, but the guy nodded anyway. Davy handed Mr. Sympathy a tip that he tried to refuse, but when he saw how miserable Davy was, he mouthed a *thank you* and accepted it with a smile.

Davy made his way to the stairs but came up short when someone tapped him on the shoulder. He turned and died a little inside when he saw it was one of Gavin's friends. The guy's smile was welcoming and kind, excited even. If Davy remembered right, this was Sean. He was a cute Latino with wavy black hair and a cinnamon complexion, and he was easily the thinnest of them all. But he was always nice, so Davy couldn't be a dick and tell him to fuck off.

Sean pointed at him enthusiastically. "Oh my God! I knew it was you! Davy, right?"

Davy nodded. "Yep. It's me. Sean?"

"Right! Guess we're hard to forget when we drag that idiot around, eh?"

Davy's buzz was obviously not totally gone because he smiled openly at that.

Another of Gavin's friends walked up, but Davy couldn't remember this guy's name, so he just said, "How's it going, chocolate soda?"

The guy held out his fist for a bump. "It's Mason."

Davy awkwardly bumped fists with Mason, and Sean said, "Holy balls! Gav is gonna shit when he sees you!"

Davy blanched. "Uh. I was just headed out."

Sean and Mason laughed.

"You can't leave without letting him know you're here, man. It'll be awesome. He'll swoon all night and we will give him so much shit," Mason said.

Davy shook his head. He couldn't get the "hell, no" out, so that would have to suffice.

"Davy, you have to! You'd really be doing *us* a favor."

Sean looked like a kid who was plotting against his older brother. Davy looked over their shoulders. The go-go boy and Gavin were still sucking face, and the go-go boy's Andrew Christians were doing nothing to hide his hard-on. The hard-on Gavin had his hand on.

"I think he's doing just fine." Davy knew it was bitchy, but he was done with this and just wanted to go home. It was his turn to give the I-told-you-so look when Sean and Mason saw what Gavin was doing on the dance floor.

They both wore grimaces when they turned back to him.

"I'm outta here." He bolted before either of them could stop him. He thought he heard them call for him, but he didn't turn back. He just kept on down the stairs and out of the club. He'd embarrassed himself enough for one night.

CHAPTER THREE

GAVIN CHECKED himself in the mirror of the club bathroom and set himself to rights. He was just thankful he hadn't lost his favorite beanie this time. It was almost tradition now. He'd gotten to the point where he'd bought several that looked alike because every time he went out dancing these days he'd leave it in someone's car, lose it while he was dancing, or a trick would walk off with it.

Speaking of hookups, tonight's boy had been pretty special. He had a pleasant ache in his ass that'd be reminding him of how *talented* the dancer boy—Juan?—had been. He couldn't help but smirk at himself in the mirror. Add the go-go boys to the long list of reasons Gavin would never miss his mother's home in Maine. But he sure as hell didn't want to think about any of that right now. That'd be a good way to fuck up the pleasant buzz he had from alcohol and good sex.

As he exited the club, the balmy spring air whipped his face, and he breathed in the smells coming from the ubiquitous hot-dog stands. He lit a cigarette and inhaled the soothing burn of nicotine, the cherry on the top of his buzz. He felt loose and relaxed as he watched the drunk gays and their hags stumble around in slutty clothes as they caught cabs and town cars or made their way to one of the many options for food to soak up the alcohol they'd consumed. He was soothed by the energy of all of the people out on the streets. He'd never felt as at home as he did on a Saturday night when downtown was lit up and everyone was laughing and happy after a night out, buzzing with life even at 2:00 a.m.

He pulled his phone out to dial a cab, but a message from Sean telling him to meet them at their favorite after-hours pizza place caught his attention. Sean had sent it only ten minutes earlier, so he hadn't missed them and there was a slice of pesto pizza calling his name.

When Gavin sat down at their booth in the pizza place they always ate at after hitting the club, Sean's first words to him were "Dude, you are *such* an idiot." Mason had a bite of pizza in his mouth, but he spoke an emphatic "uh-huh" around the half-masticated glob of pesto and crust. The other guys, Nate and Devon, shrugged as though they were as clueless as Gavin. He reared back.

"What the hell?" His friends looked serious. He was expecting the usual ragging about being a slut, but this was new.

"You have no idea, Gav." Mason shook his head and took another huge bite of his pizza.

Gavin was bemused every time Mason stuffed his face when he was drunk. Ah, the joys of trying to sober the fuck up.

"What are you guys talking about?" Gavin snatched a breadstick off Nate's plate. "If it's because he was a go-go boy, that's rude. He has to make a living too."

"We're not talking about your slutty little friend. We're talking about your shy little crush." Sean leveled his gaze at Gavin.

Gavin drew his eyebrows together in confusion.

"Your slutty ways have caught up with you, Gavvy-kins," Mason said, shaking his head in… was that disgust?

"What the fuck, guys? Harsh much?" He'd never admit they were really hurting his feelings. Could be because he knew what they said was the truth. He couldn't help thinking bitterly that he'd gotten his reputation as a total slut honestly. Sean smacked him on the back of his head and he flinched away with an "ouch!"

"You know that 'piece' you've been chasing, aka crushing on hardcore? The guy from Bart's?"

Gavin couldn't help but smile at the mention of the blond jock he'd been playing cat and mouse with for months now. "Yeah. Soda Shop Davy?"

All the guys snorted collectively and Mason shook his head sorrowfully.

"Yes. The one and the same," Sean said.

"Why?" He wished they'd just spit it out already. He started thinking of blond hair, blue eyes, and a firm jaw with a baby face and lickable pink lips. And don't forget those biceps that were just right. Not too beefy but enough to show the guy did some working out.

Sean frowned at Gavin, wiping the smile from his face. "You blew your chance officially."

"Spit it out!" Nate and Gavin said in unison.

"I'm confused" was all Devon could manage to say through his alcohol-induced haze.

Sean's look at Devon was not polite. "You're always confused. The alcohol just renders you completely worthless."

"I know, right!" Devon laughed as though he'd just said the funniest thing ever.

Everyone stared at him for a minute.

"Anyway," Gavin said, returning all attention to Sean and Mason.

"He was at the club tonight, Gavin," Mason said.

Gavin perked up. "Oh, shit! No way! Why didn't you guys tell me?"

"Well, we tried to get him to come talk to you, but he'd unfortunately already seen you groping thong-boy's schlong in front of the whole world," Sean said sardonically.

Nate gave a groan of sympathy as Gavin dropped his head with a thud on the table. "I'd say that ship has officially sailed."

"Shame, too. We'd noticed him earlier but didn't know it was him. He was definitely working up the nerve to come holla at you." Mason burped loudly as if that added something to the statement. "Way to fail."

"Why me?" Gavin's voice was muffled by the table.

"I'm sorry, Oh Slutty One. What was that?"

Leave it to Nate to goad the shit on. Devon just started giggling again. They all turned to stare at him for a quiet moment as he entertained himself in his corner of the booth.

"So what should I do?" Gavin knew he sounded desperate, but that was one piece of ass he'd been chasing far too long to see his chances vanish like this. If he was totally honest, the guy had almost become an obsession. It was those guileless blue eyes and that baby face he thought of before he fell asleep at night. He even saw them in his mind when other guys got him off. It was fucked up, but he *was* fucked up, so that made sense.

Sean patted Gavin's shoulder. "I'm afraid you had one very small window here and you slammed that motherfucker good tonight."

"On your dick. Hard. I'm surprised you didn't feel it."

"Thanks for the visual, Mase," Gavin snapped. He was feeling sorry for himself, but he'd done this to himself. *Fuck, fuck, fuck.*

He had to figure out a way to fix this. He needed one good go at Davy. He definitely needed to get that drug out of his system. Especially if chasing that ass had him this twisted up. He didn't have time for this bullshit. "I'll fix this." He sounded much surer than he felt.

Everyone gave him skeptical smirks. Devon started laughing hysterically again.

Nate pointed at the cackling Devon. "What he said."

GAVIN STUMBLED upstairs into the kitchen the next morning. He had a fully functional kitchenette in his mother-in-law suite in the basement of his grandfather's house, but the old man made better coffee. He poured himself a cup of the reviving nectar and sat down at the small table in the breakfast nook.

His grandfather looked up from his Sunday paper and immediately caught that something was amiss. "What'd you do?"

Gavin was mildly offended. "Why do you think I did something?"

"You look like you stuck your pecker in a blender, boy. I know you well enough to know that means you did something dumb."

Gavin wanted to deny any wrongdoing, but he knew it'd be futile. His grandfather really did know him too well. In fact, Raymond Marshall was his best friend in the whole world. Had been since he was a young boy. So he would know.

"Come out with it. I want to finish this crossword before I'm in my grave."

Gavin scowled. "Don't joke like that, Ray."

The old man laughed. Laughed! What the hell?

"Then don't keep me waiting."

Gavin gave his best put-upon sigh. "I fucked things up with this guy I've been after for a while."

"Well, that's no surprise with the way you go through 'em."

"Hey!" Gavin puffed his chest up indignantly, but his grandfather gave him a significant stare that dared him to challenge the truth.

"What'd you do to the guy? It wasn't another one of those ga-ga boys was it?"

"Go-go. It's go-go, Ray." Gavin had explained this enough times that he figured the old guy was just messing with him. He wasn't sure how to explain what had happened. No explanation Gavin tried in his head made him sound good. But it wasn't as if he'd cheated on the guy. Quite frankly, he was tired of being the butt of his friends' jokes. They acted as though it was some big shame that he wasn't afraid to get laid when nature called. He knew better. He was a man, after all. Not like he was as bad as his mom. *Am I?*

"Well?" Ray set his paper down and continued staring at Gavin. "Is this a whiskey conversation?"

"It's not even noon!" Gavin couldn't help but laugh. His grandfather called whiskey the truth serum. They'd had whiskey when it was time to talk about everything from his cancer prognosis to Gavin's mom. Ray wasn't an alcoholic by any means, he was just old-school. Cigars, whiskey, booze, and "fine tail" were all a part of enjoying life if he didn't have much time left.

"Because you've never been drunk before noon." Ray had a point there. He stood, groaning as he stretched old joints, and shuffled over to the cabinet where they kept the hard stuff. He returned to the table with two glasses and plopped them down along with a bottle of Jack.

Gavin smiled fondly at his grandfather. He was once a tall, burly guy, but after a bout with cancer, he was smaller but still had that strong personality.

Ray caught his grandson looking at him and harrumphed. "Stop writing my eulogy in your head, boy, and divvy up that whiskey."

Gavin sighed again but did as he was told.

They sipped their drinks for a minute before Ray decided to break out his deck of playing cards, announcing, "Rummy." He started dealing out the cards. This was what they spent most of their free time doing. Whiskey and cards. Sometimes just them, sometimes Ray's friends. His group of buddies were all retired cops who'd worked together in the Seattle PD over the last forty years. They were a wild crew, and they all spoiled Gavin. He knew he was lucky. When shit hit the fan back home in Maine, his grandfather hadn't batted an eyelash before he'd told him to hightail it to the West Coast.

They played two hands that Ray won, of course, and went through about three rocks glasses apiece before Gavin finally spoke.

"Am I like her?" It was a quiet question.

Ray dropped his cards and looked at Gavin as though he'd asked the dumbest question he'd ever heard. "Boy, on your worst day you're better than she ever was on her best. What makes you think something so foolish?"

"I think I messed something up. Something that didn't exist yet, but something that could have been real."

"Thinking with your pecker got you in a bind, huh?"

Gavin thought there was a better way to say it but had to concede. "Pretty much."

"Well, is it worth keeping it in your pants and trying again?"

Gavin remembered seeing through the store window the shy smile Davy had given that little girl the other day, and turned over all the reasons it'd be stupid to put all his chips on such an uncertain bet. "I don't know. Like I said, we didn't have anything at all. I've been flirting, he's been telling me to fuck off."

Ray chuckled. "Well, that's the oldest story in the book. You want what you can't have. Again, is it worth it? Does it hurt your heart or does it hurt your balls?"

Gavin choked on the whiskey he'd been sipping. Fuck if that didn't burn his throat. "Fuck!" he rasped. Ray laughed a belly laugh, and through the burn of the whiskey Gavin still felt that warm laugh down into his soul. He didn't know what he'd do without the old bastard, and he said as much.

"You'd never win a hand of poker in your life." Ray started dealing cards again. "Way I see it, you've used that thing between your legs enough to know the difference in whether you're wanting with it or wanting with that thing beating in your scrawny chest."

Gavin stewed on that. He pulled out his memories of Davy and played them over in his head. The smiles, the banter, the blushes. Yeah. He barely knew Soda Shop Boy, but something about Davy was different. Or maybe he just needed a good roll in the sack with the guy.

"Lord, boy, stop your drooling and play cards. Shameless."

Gavin gave his cockiest grin and pointed at Ray with his cards. "I learned from the best."

Ray gave a sniff that was much daintier than a man of his gruff nature should be able to muster. "It's your go. Lay down a damn card."

Gavin did as he was told but never stopped smiling.

CHAPTER
FOUR

GAVIN HAD been so lost in thought he didn't hear Sean's approach, so the fingers snapping in his face to get his attention almost got broken when he gripped them and jerked the offender to the ground. When he realized the person blinking up at him with owlish eyes was his best friend, he grimaced. "Oh shit, dude. I'm so sorry." He offered his hand to help Sean up, but Sean swatted it away.

Sean scowled while he dusted himself off. "Well, I see you're in a good mood today," Sean said.

Gavin, feeling sufficiently chastened, held out the coffee he'd picked up for his friend, using it now as a peace offering. "Sorry. I was a million miles away."

"No shit," Sean groused as he headed toward one of the benches.

Gavin hated to leave his perch overlooking Elliot Bay. The park was teeming with tourists. It was a beautiful spring day boasting a rare eighty degrees and a clear sky. Losing himself staring out over the sparkling water of the sound had been a rare moment of peace. His thoughts hadn't turned maudlin. He was ashamed to say that more often than not he was throwing a pity party for himself these days. He hated it. That wasn't him.

"Yo, Gav. You in there?" Sean was looking at him expectantly.

He hadn't realized he'd wandered off in his mind again.

"Oh, yeah. Sorry." He followed Sean's lead and took a seat on an empty bench by a group of homeless people who were passing around a bottle of booze and stretching out in the sun like lounging house cats with a communal bowl of cream.

"I asked how your gramps is doing. You said he had an appointment with his doctor today."

Gavin watched a toothless woman take a long pull from the bottle of cheap vodka she was sharing with her disenfranchised crew. He couldn't bring himself to look at Sean, not wanting to see any pity in his expression. Sean had been around through the lengthy battle Ray had waged against his pancreatic cancer.

"Oncologist again. He wouldn't let me go." Gavin knew his expression was probably bitter, but he was annoyed that he'd been banned from the appointment. "Now that he's finished radiation, they're gonna tell him what the latest tests have to say. We'll know where we stand after this."

"You know he wants you there. He's just trying to protect you from all this crap."

"It's hard, but he's all I've got. I wanna know what we're up against."

"Dude, that's why he went alone. He knows if it's bad news it'll kill you. You've fought the whole way with him, so maybe he didn't want this one to be your burden to bear too." Sean patted Gavin's shoulder.

Gavin appreciated what his friend was saying. He was just scared. Not that he'd ever admit that.

He shrugged Sean off and chugged the last of his coffee. "Wanna go to Bart's with me after work?"

"You have no shame."

"So I've heard." He crushed his cup, balled it up, and tossed it like a basketball into the trash can across the path from their bench, sinking it in one shot. He threw a cocky smirk Sean's way.

"You know I know you well enough to know you're not the badass you think you are." Sean just shook his head.

Yeah, Sean knew more than anyone that three-fourths of Gavin's swagger was posturing against the world that had fucked him raw most of his life. But he was no victim. When he'd moved to Seattle four years earlier, he'd promised himself he was gonna fuck the world right back. He'd met Sean his first night at the gay bar. Sean had seen Gavin leaving the bathroom with the first of many conquests, laughed, and commented on how fucked up his hat hair was. That was when he'd lost his first beanie. He was pissed, and not just at being picked on. But Sean saw past the chip on his shoulder and ignored that. They'd gone out for pizza after that, and Sean introduced Gavin to his friends Nate, Mason, and Devon, and the rest was history. He'd lived it up and enjoyed school and hanging out with the guys when they weren't working at the market. So far he'd made life his bitch.

Until that one day last year when Ray came home, pulled out the whiskey, and announced he had cancer. Inoperable. Gavin hated that word.

He couldn't sit anymore, so he jumped up and walked back over to the rails where he'd been looking out over the flowing traffic on the Alaskan Way Viaduct and the glimmer of the sun off the water of the bay on the other side. In his peripheral vision, he saw Sean lean on the rail next to him, squinting his dark eyes against the sun. Gavin could appreciate how attractive Sean was with his fine Latino features. If Gavin was the dating type, he might even have found that Sean was the perfect boyfriend. He was a genuinely good guy. But Gavin wasn't the dating type and he just couldn't think of Sean that way.

"So you're not throwing in the towel, huh?" Sean teased, obviously trying to lighten the mood. Good ol' Sean.

"No way! That's one Grade-A piece of ass. That'd be like the 'Hawks giving up on a chance at the Super Bowl."

Sean laughed, and Gavin knew it was at him, not with him. Douche. "Gavin, man, maybe you should try just being the guy's friend." Gavin looked at him incredulously, but before he could respond, Sean threw his hands up to silence him. "I'm just sayin'. The guy seems to be short on friends. He was all alone at the club the other night. I saw him sitting in the booth by himself for a long time before I figured out it was him. That's just sad, dude. Quiet as he is, it don't surprise me, though."

Gavin weighed this information for a moment, trying to think how he could best use it to his advantage. Sean punched him in the shoulder. "You're such a dick, Gavin. I know exactly what you're thinking, and it's shitty."

"You have no idea what I'm thinking." Gavin rubbed his shoulder. That punch hurt, dammit.

"No? You're not thinking you'll try to be his friend then make your move when he's all comfortable with you?"

Shit. Maybe Sean knew him too well. "The best sex happens among friends." Gavin thought it sounded reasonable.

"You're such an ass. And if you ever put the moves on me, I'll break your dick off."

Gavin had a good comeback for that, but before he could get it out, there was a commotion that got his and Sean's attention. Some dickhead in a suit was yelling at a cute guy for bumping into him. As crowded as this part of town got it was just a part of life, and it looked like the cute guy had dropped his bag, his papers and books scattered everywhere. Sean mumbled something about the guy being an asshole just as it dawned on Gavin that the cute guy fumbling to pick up his scattered belongings while stammering apologies was Soda Shop Davy. He was moving toward the action, which was drawing more than a few stares, before he could stop himself. He may be a dick himself, but he'd never treat a stranger like that. Then the guy started kicking at Davy's books and putting on some pathetic display he'd never have gotten away with if it had been any other guy on the street.

As Gavin bolted toward Davy and the guy, Sean called him back, but he had one objective. He snatched the weasel in the suit by his designer collar and reared back to hit the fucker in the mouth. Before he could let his fist fly, a hand gripped his bicep firmly. He snapped his head around and was face-to-face with Davy, who was shaking his head and saying, "No, Gavin. No, no, no."

"This fucker giving you trouble, Davy?"

"Gavin, stop. It's okay. I ran into him. It was just an accident."

"Looked like he was fucking with you to me." Gavin snarled in the weasel's face. The guy was cowering, eyes wide with his hands in front of his face. Gavin had at least five inches on the asshole—hell, Davy did too, for that matter.

"Gav, c'mon, man. This is not worth it." Sean put his hand on Gavin's other shoulder.

Gavin breathed heavily for a moment and tried to get a grip. Why was he being so protective? He was acting as though he was standing up for his boyfriend. The word *mine* had tasted bad in his mouth as he ran to Davy's defense. He just wanted to fuck Davy, not marry him.

He let the guy go with a hard shove that made Weasel Man drop his briefcase. "Learn some fucking manners, asshole!" He snarled at the guy again as the dude made a hasty retreat. There was a smattering of applause, but there were more people leaning in whispering to their friends and staring. There were also a few Asian tourists with large smiles and snapping cameras. He was apparently more interesting than the chick who'd painted her body in bronze and pretended to be a statue just ten feet from him. She looked at him as though he'd snatched a john from her. *Who gets mad at someone for doing a good deed?* "Get a real job, lady." He flipped her off.

Behind him, Sean sounded exasperated with a "Nice, Gavin. Real nice." But the chick just flipped him off right back and wandered off to greener pastures.

"You okay, Davy?" He squatted to help pick up the errant papers and books. A few had shoe prints from where Weasel Man had stepped on them. Gavin wanted to chase the douchebag down and beat his ass. It looked as though he'd damaged some textbooks, and Lord knew those weren't cheap.

"Yeah. It was my fault."

Davy was mumbling, so Gavin barely heard it, but when he figured out what Davy said, his hackles rose.

He grabbed Davy by the collar of his powder-blue polo shirt. *Damn, that color brings out his eyes.* "Get one thing straight, Davy. This is the market. People run into each other all the time. His fancy suit didn't give him the right to talk down to you like that. So don't let me hear you say it was your fault again. You had nothing to apologize for."

Davy's pupils dilated, and he licked his rosy bottom lip with the tip of his tongue. Gavin's cock was very interested in seeing Davy do that again. Damn that kid for being so hot. And if Gavin wasn't mistaken, Davy was just as affected by his close proximity. He quirked an eyebrow at Davy, then let him go and smoothed out his shirt for him.

"Okay...." Sean's eyes lit up, bemused. Damn. Gavin had forgotten he was there. "While you guys are macking on each other in public, I'm gonna head to work. I'm already late." Davy blushed and busied himself shoving things back into his messenger bag. "Oh no. Don't stop on my account. The Asian ladies aren't finished taking pictures of you." Sean pointed to where the camera-wielding tourists were still tittering together, watching them.

Davy's face turned a nice shade of crimson as he turned his back to the ladies. Gavin and Sean traded a look of amusement and tried to hold back laughter.

Gavin was about to head over to the stack of papers and books he'd gathered when he saw the bright-yellow flyer on top. "Hey, you like the Jawbreakers?" He was surprised. Davy didn't seem like the house-music, club-kid type. Davy snatched the stack from Gavin with a "thanks," but Gavin saw an opening and he was gonna take it. He had just made a fool of himself for Davy, so the least Davy could do was answer a simple question.

"You going to the show?" Gavin persisted.

Davy was hesitant, but he eventually shrugged. "I'm not sure. I like them, but I think the show is sold out."

Gavin gave Davy his most winning smile. "You're in luck. I'm going and a friend backed out. I happen to have an extra ticket. You should come with." Davy opened his mouth to protest, but Gavin spoke over his objection. "It'll just go to waste, and I don't want to go alone." Davy's expression was dubious at best. "Just as friends! Don't make me go alone. None of my friends like dubstep. You owe me for being your knight in shining armor, anyway." Davy scoffed at that. "Please?" Gavin tried for an angelic expression that got him an eye roll from Davy, but he got those from Davy quite often, so he wasn't discouraged. "If you have a horrible time, I'll never ask you to go anywhere with me again."

Davy was clearly calling bullshit on that one. "Seriously?"

"Cross my heart." He made an X over his heart.

"Okay." Davy looked as though he couldn't believe he'd agreed to it, then nodded as though he'd accepted his fate.

"Awesome!" Gavin gave Davy a playful punch to the shoulder.

"But I'll meet you there, okay?"

Gavin preferred picking the guy up, but he'd play by Davy's rules just this once. "Perfect. I'll be waiting outside at seven thirty."

Davy nodded again. "Okay. I'll be there." He put his bag back over his shoulder and took a step back from Gavin. "Well, I should get to work too. You guys have a good day. I'll, uh, see you Thursday, then." He turned and headed off down the sidewalk at a brisk pace. *Damn, those jeans fit that ass just right.* Gavin's cock agreed as it plumped in his shorts.

When Davy was out of earshot, Gavin gave a triumphant "Yessss!"

"So I'm guessing I'm out of a ticket, huh?"

Gavin jumped at the sound of Sean's voice. "Dude, you scared the hell out of me!" Sean had his hands crossed over his chest, but he didn't seem pissed. "Er. Yeah. I'll make it up to you, though."

Sean waved him off. "Don't worry about it. Just don't fuck up with that guy, okay." Gavin tried his best "who, me?" routine, but Sean didn't bite. "You're such an ass," Sean said affectionately. And with that, he left Gavin at the mercy of the Asian ladies who were looking at him with flirting eyes and rosy cheeks.

Being the smart-ass he was, he did the only thing that seemed appropriate now.

He took a bow.

CHAPTER
FIVE

THE CONCERT was in the Industrial District in a converted warehouse. The neighborhood was close to the water and had a dingy covering of dirt over all the buildings that made everything look gray. Davy had never been a fan of the area. There wasn't much to do other than go to one of the few bars, which were mostly populated with frat-boys, metalheads, or Seattle's version of rednecks. He hadn't even heard of the large club the concert was housed in until he saw one of his favorite bands would be performing there tonight.

Davy still wasn't sure why in the hell he'd said yes to Gavin. That feeling grew with each passing moment. He was nervous, trying to fend off a panic attack. Not only had he agreed to be around a ridiculous amount of people, but he would be there with Gavin. And none of the people going in there looked like Davy's kind of crowd. Not that anyone was really his kind of crowd, but these were hard-core club kids wearing bright colors, short skirts, stilettos, and random accessories that had blinking lights in them. *Hope there are no epileptics attending tonight.*

Adding to his nerves, Gavin said they were there just as friends, but Davy wasn't sure he trusted that. Although, after being sufficiently emasculated in public by that jackass in the park on Monday morning, and then again when Gavin swooped in to defend him, he couldn't imagine Gavin saw him as anything other than the pitiful creature he'd come across as.

Not that he wanted Gavin to think of him any other way. Well, maybe not the pitiful part, but he didn't exactly trust guys enough to want to date anyone, and Gavin didn't have a trustworthy bone in his body. The guy may be sex from head to toe, but that predatory gleam to his eyes left Davy feeling let down when he'd realized Gavin had only helped him in the park so he could manipulate him into a date. He'd almost allowed himself to believe Gavin was actually defending him because he liked him. But the shameless way he'd goaded Davy into coming to the concert with him was a neon sign saying "I'm gonna make you my bitch."

So that's why you took an hour to get ready and showed up early?

"Shut up, you." *Oh, now you look crazy fussing at yourself.*

He glanced around to make sure no one had heard his moment of weirdness. He owned his eccentricity, wore it like a badge, but he didn't like the idea of a stranger having him carted off in the jacket with the arms tied behind the back because he was fighting with himself.

As if Davy wasn't feeling dumb enough for being so early, Gavin was ten minutes late. *Fuck this.* He shoved his hands in his pockets. This was ridiculous and he was not sticking around. He'd just tell Gavin something had come up—if he ever saw him again. He was tired as hell anyway. He'd been late with an assignment and that had set off his anxiety. That's why Davy never procrastinated. Last-minute pressure always flustered him, and then the realization he was flustered would set off a freak-out that tumbled over into a crippling inability to function—a fucked-up domino effect that could be easily avoided by just doing shit in a timely manner.

Instead, he'd remembered his late assignment while working the night before and flipped out while trying to close down and had just barely survived closing. The repetitive routine of counting down and cleaning had eased his nerves enough to get him home and in bed. Which was where he really wanted to be now.

Only he didn't get so far as across the street when he spotted Gavin loping toward him decked out, looking good enough to lick. He even made smoking look sexy. And Davy *hated* cigarettes. Davy couldn't help but stare at Gavin's easy swagger as he crossed the street, jaywalking. The guy didn't follow any rules, even simple ones, did he?

Gavin drew nearer, and Davy's heart thudded harder and his cock started pointing toward the man as if attracted to its polar north. The guy was fucking devastating in a pair of straight-legged black jeans, white high tops, and a gray Henley, buttons open to reveal a chest tattoo. And of course he wore his beanie. Did he ever take it off? The tattoos on his arms and his James Dean bad-boy looks were getting him stares from more than just one passing person—male and female. But that damn smug smirk that seemed to be his trademark quirked up on the edge of his mouth as soon as his gaze lighted on Davy. Davy felt that goddamned smirk down to his toes.

"Heya, Davy," Gavin drawled.

Davy almost came in his chinos when Gavin took a final drag from his cigarette, holding it between his thumb and his forefinger before flicking it on the ground and stamping it out. That mouth was lethal.

"Litter much," Davy scolded. *Smooth.*

Gavin cackled and dismissed the words, scanning the crowd gathering at the door of the club. He didn't look impressed. "What are them lame dudes doing here?" He pointed to a group of guys who looked as though they'd tried too hard to emulate the cast of *Jersey Shore*.

Davy didn't feel quite so lame now. His black V-neck and chinos looked *GQ* compared to those idiots with their popped-collar Abercrombie shirts and orange spray tans.

"We call that the douche patrol. What, did every freshman at U-Dub decide to hit this show tonight?"

Davy shrugged. Gavin appraised him for a minute. His stony-faced scrutiny was almost unbearable. Davy felt as though he could finally breathe again when Gavin went back to scanning the crowd of concertgoers.

"Uh, as much as I like this group, those douches look like they'll get the cops called on this gig and I hate this part of town. Would you oppose ditching and doing something else?"

Davy agreed with Gavin's assessment, but he was wary of the invitation to do anything else. Partly because he wasn't sure whether Gavin actually didn't want to deal with the crowd or if he could tell just how uncomfortable Davy was. He hoped like hell it wasn't the latter. He was tired of embarrassing himself in front of Gavin only to have Gavin come to the rescue.

"Like what?" His tone was so dubious Gavin gave a hearty laugh. Davy couldn't deny that it warmed him inside. It was such an honest laugh, and Gavin's face was open and relaxed like it had been at the club when he was with his friends and unaware of the eyes on him.

"Well, we're all dressed up, may as well have somewhere to go." Gavin pulled out his phone and started typing. After a moment the text-message tone sounded and he smiled. "Hey, Sean says karaoke is on over at The Place. He and Mason are there."

Davy was really unsure. He did feel better knowing that they wouldn't be there alone, and he had spent a lot of time getting ready. And if he was perfectly honest, he had been looking forward to actually spending a night out with another person, even if it was Gavin with his leering and flirting that just never turned off.

"Davy! C'mon. Drinks, watching drunk gays trying to hit Whitney's high notes."

Davy almost gagged at the puppy-dog eyes Gavin attempted to sway him with. Granted, they were really pretty brown puppy-dog eyes, but that innocent look was in direct contradiction to the bad-boy thing Gavin was trying for. Davy wondered which one was the real Gavin, which made him even more wary of the guy.

Gavin sighed. "Okay. How about this? Come for an hour. If you hate it, I'll tell 'em I hit on you and you stormed out because I'm a major dickhead." Davy felt himself giving in. Gavin obviously saw a crack in the façade, so he decided to move in for the kill. "I mean, you look hella sexy tonight. May as well show off that ass in those chinos. That should not be hidden from the world."

Davy blushed. "Okay, gah. Just don't say any more shit like that, okay?" Gavin laughed again, and Davy couldn't imagine saying anything other than a resounding yes to any question Gavin might ask if he kept looking at Davy with that brilliant light in his eyes.

And you thought you were above being led around by your dick.

"Didn't I tell you to shut up?" Davy snapped.

Gavin stopped laughing, face displaying total surprise. Davy stammered through an apology but couldn't think of anything that made him sound less crazy, so he settled for "Sorry. Uh, let's just get going."

He mentally kicked his own ass the whole way to the bus stop.

GAVIN WAS many things, but stupid he was not. He could tell Davy was not feeling the concert at all. He wasn't impressed with the crowd himself, but Davy was almost vibrating with his need to get the hell out of there. He was glad he'd messaged Sean, because twenty minutes in the bar and a cocktail later, Davy had loosened up a little. Sean and Davy seemed to get along well. Davy was talkative with him.... If you could call it talkative. Talkative for Davy, anyway.

It wasn't hard to figure out that Davy didn't get out a lot, but after about his fourth vodka and cranberry and a group shot of tequila, he'd confirmed it by saying, "I never do this, guys." He was still shy as hell, even drunk, but he thanked them for inviting him out. Gavin wished he could be as good with Davy as Sean was. Sean was patient and asked the right questions. Then there was Mason whose enthusiasm was infectious, so he had Davy almost bouncy and laughing openly at his antics. Gavin didn't mind too much, though. While Sean had Davy talking about how horrible it was that some queen murdered an Usher song—"How dare they give him a mic!" *Damn, Davy has fangs. Store that away for later—* Gavin got a good look at Davy. And damn, was that boy sexier than Gavin would have guessed in his uniform khakis and Bart's Soda Shop T-shirt.

Davy's black V-neck was obviously just an undershirt. It was thin and looked soft, much like Davy. Oh yes, Davy had muscles in all the right places. His pecs were nicely rounded and his biceps bulged just enough to stretch the short sleeves. But he was still soft. He looked like someone you'd hug for hours and never get tired of it. He obviously played some kind of sport or worked out regularly, because that was not a body genetically gifted. And damn if Gavin wasn't having the hardest time keeping his hands off it.

He was annoyed when Sean looked at his phone and announced it was time for him to go, and Mason followed suit. He wasn't finished drinking in Davy. He needed more time. He knew no matter how drunk the kid got, he'd never get laid. Dammit if that didn't make him like Davy more. Who'd've known scruples would be a turn-on for Gavin Walker?

After everyone shared bro hugs and agreed they'd do it again, it was just Davy and Gavin again. Gavin paid their tab, telling Davy not to worry about it. "Well, since you paid the tab, let me buy dinner. Is there anything open? I'm starving." Gavin almost tripped over his own feet, shocked that Davy wasn't running as fast as possible from spending time alone with him.

"Uh, Dick's is open."

Davy sniggered. Oh yeah, he was good and toasted. "Dick's?"

"That's very mature of you, David."

Davy cocked his head, looking at Gavin strangely. "It's just Davy. No David." It was delivered very matter-of-factly. Gavin wasn't sure if he'd just been told off or if it was just a friendly correction.

"Sorry."

"No. It's cool. You wouldn't be the first to make the mistake."

"Well, *Davy*, do you want Dick's?"

"Um, I guess. I've never eaten there."

Gavin grabbed his heart in mock offense. "And you say you've lived here your whole life?"

"Born and raised here in King County."

"And you've never had Dick's? It's, like, one of the treasures of Seattle!"

Davy glared at him quickly, then seemed to pull his shy façade back over him like a comfortable blanket. *Shit.* "Hey, Davy, what's that all about? What'd I say?"

Davy chewed his tongue for a moment before he responded. "It's me, really. I've never been good with getting teased. I don't read social cues very well. I, uh, didn't get to be around a lot of people my age until I got my job at the soda shop."

"Oh?" Gavin didn't want to fuck up again. He'd been waiting forever for some little tidbit about this man. He wasn't sure why Davy was so intriguing. Maybe it *was* because he couldn't have him. Normally he wouldn't look twice at someone as shy as this guy was. But he wanted to know Davy, and if it required him keeping his fool mouth closed for once in his damn life, he could do it. So all he did was start walking in the direction of Dick's waving for Davy to follow.

Davy was silent for the rest of the walk. He didn't say anything again until he requested a large order of fries and a chocolate shake. Gavin somehow didn't imagine it was going to help his libido any to watch Davy suck a straw for the next fifteen minutes.

He was right. Those rosy lips wrapped around the straw, Davy's cheeks caving in as he sucked, and Gavin almost had to excuse himself to the bathroom. Then Davy's wicked tongue would sneak out to lick the salt off his lips and there was no need for the bathroom. He was fairly certain he'd creamed his jeans. Now a cigarette and a bed would complete the night.

How in the hell did Davy have that kind of power over him?

They ate silently, Gavin watching the crowd thin until there were only two couples other than them. He and Davy finished eating, so he collected their trash and dumped it into the bin. He turned to say something to Davy, but he hadn't followed. He was still sitting in the booth, eyes downcast. Gavin felt a frown pulling the corners of his mouth. *Please don't let him be a crybaby drunk.*

"Hey, Davy? Ready to go?"

"Can we just sit here for a minute?" Gavin studied Davy for a moment, not sure what to make of him. Davy took it as a no and started stammering. "Never mind. It was dumb. Sorry." He'd not looked up once since he'd asked if they could stay, and tried to shuffle out of the booth. Gavin placed a hand on his chest and pushed him back down into the booth.

"Dude, chill. I got nothing but time, 'kay? It's all good."

Davy gazed out the window looking particularly miserable, embarrassed.

"What's wrong?" Gavin hated to push, but he really wanted to figure out these weird triggers of Davy's.

"Sorry." Davy finally looked at him, eyes a bit watery. "I promise I'm not a crier when I drink. I just don't do well with people. I hate embarrassing myself."

Gavin placed his hand over Davy's on the table and tried to sound as encouraging as possible. "You did nothing embarrassing. I just couldn't tell if something was wrong. You seem bummed. That's all."

Davy stared at Gavin's hand covering his for a long minute, then pulled his away and put it in his lap. "I was homeschooled. I couldn't remember if I told you that."

"No. You didn't. That's cool." It explained it a little, but Gavin knew plenty of homeschooled kids who were way less shy than Davy.

"Not really. It wasn't cool. I wanted to go to school." Guilt flashed over Davy's face. "Homeschooling would have been cool, but my mom wouldn't really let me do any of the group stuff."

"Why so?"

Davy grimaced. "She had panic attacks. Uh, something bad happened and she stopped leaving the house. Therefore, neither did I."

The pieces fell into place so loudly in Gavin's mind that it sounded like a game of Bunko rattling in his brain. "Is that who you live with now?"

Pure sorrow surrounded Davy. From his posture to his frown. "No. She died about a year ago. Aneurysm. It's just me now."

Oh, Davy.

"I'm so sorry."

Davy's chin trembled, but he never shed a tear. "Thanks. It was sudden, so I'm still caught off guard by the fact she's gone, sometimes."

Gavin didn't know what it was like to miss your mother. He would never miss his. He was glad it wouldn't eat at him like it did Davy, but he knew he'd break like this if something happened to Ray. He definitely understood the loss. "What was her name?"

"Mona." Davy didn't look up from his hands in his lap. "She was a good mom. I wish she'd done some stuff different, but she was good."

"I'm sure she was." Gavin hated seeing Davy so down, so he thought it'd be wise to direct the conversation back to where they'd started. "So what do you do? Sit in your apartment by yourself?" That seemed so sad.

"I work a lot, as you well know"—that was pointedly accusatory—"and I do online classes. I don't get much chance to meet people, but I'm sure you've noticed I'm not great with people anyways, so I don't ever know what to do when I get the chance to try to be friends with someone." He chewed on his tongue, obviously a nervous habit, then laughed derisively. "Like now. You guys were great. You only hit on me the one time. Sean and Mason did their best to help me fit in, and here I am being a freak and dumping my shit on you."

"Davy, that's what friends are for." *Friends don't want to kiss it all better, though, Gavin.*

"I guess, but I still feel like an idiot."

"Don't. Just, if you need to talk or just need to sit somewhere and be quiet but have someone else around, I'll be here, 'kay. Just a friend. No judgment."

Davy gave a small smile. It wasn't incredibly encouraging, but it was an improvement. "Give me a sec," Gavin said. He ran to the counter and asked to borrow a pen. He pulled a napkin out of the dispenser and jotted down his number. He was surprised to find he really had no ulterior motive this time. He smiled at the girl who'd let him borrow the pen and thanked her before returning to the table and passing his number to Davy. "Use it. Please. Coffee, a movie, help with your fucking homework. Me and Sean can take you out and get you drunk. Whatever.

You want friends, you got 'em." He couldn't believe the words coming out of his mouth. No matter how sexy the guy was, he was clearly not Gavin's type and vice versa, but friends they could definitely do.

Davy looked at the napkin for a moment, then smiled sweetly. That was definitely an improvement. He folded the napkin neatly and put it away in his wallet. Gavin couldn't help but smile too. "Can we stay just a little while longer?" Davy asked quietly.

"Of course we can," Gavin said warmly. "As long as you want."

CHAPTER SIX

DAVY LOOKED longingly out the front windows of the soda shop. After a week of constant gray skies and drizzling rain, they'd had another unseasonably warm, sunny day that had given way to a beautifully clear night. Davy had picked up a second shift to help out one of the girls he worked with, so he'd been in the shop from early morning and would be around until close. He'd been alone behind the counter all day save for the hour or so that the owner, Henry, had come in. It was still off-season and a Tuesday, so even the park had been unusually empty most of the day.

He was surprised how bored he'd been without Gavin or one of his crew popping in throughout the day. Since their night out two weeks earlier, it was as if they'd come in every day to say hello, Gavin reminding him, "I only said I'd stay away if you had a horrible time." Davy had to admit he'd had a great time. He was still mortified how much the drinking had loosened his tongue, especially with Gavin. There was something else, though, about Gavin that made Davy want to open up to him some.

Davy hadn't had a friend in a long time. When Gavin stopped with the innuendos and extended an offer of friendship, Davy latched on to it like a love-starved orphan from a third-world country. He was a little embarrassed about how he'd acted at Dick's, but Gavin made a point of acting as though those last, maudlin moments at Dick's hadn't happened. Davy was eternally grateful, especially when Sean and Mason also made sure to pop in the shop on their breaks to say hi or ask if he wanted to have lunch with them. Their other friends Nate and Devon only came when it was the entire group, and Nate was a bit cold in his demeanor toward Davy. Davy wasn't sure why, but Nate made him uncomfortable. Then again, who didn't?

Gavin was his most constant visitor, though. Gavin would swagger in after class under the guise of getting peanut-butter shakes for his grandfather, but after a few days, he'd dropped the pretense and would just wander in and sit at one of the stools at the counter and talk about inconsequential things.

Davy learned a few precious details about his new friends. Since he still wasn't one for talking, they'd talk and he'd listen and smile at their stories. Sean's parents were from Columbia, but, like Davy, he'd been born and raised in Seattle. When he was annoyed he'd go on tirades in Spanish, but that was rare. Mason was from some small town in Texas and had moved up to Seattle for college but had dropped out after a year and decided not to leave. He was so laid-back Davy was surprised the guy wasn't catatonic.

Both Sean and Mason worked across the street in the market, Mason in a coffee shop and Sean in the comic store. Then there was Devon, who tossed fish. He was sexy as sin, but his permanent dopey grin and good nature made him approachable. He was, by definition, a total airhead, but he was really nice. Devon was also quiet, like Davy—well, not in a shy way, just in a man-of-few-words way.

Gavin, on the other hand, was a full-time student who lived with his grandfather after moving from Maine. He lived off some trust that he insisted wasn't impressive, but it was nice enough that he drove around in a rather large new-model Ford truck. Why he needed such a big truck in Seattle was anyone's guess.

Davy was surprised when he found out Gavin was an art major at the University of Washington. He didn't seem very artsy or like one for school, but Sean had assured Davy that Gavin was in fact in the top 10 percent of the art department as far as grades went. When he'd found that out, you could have knocked Davy over with a feather.

This had been the first day none of them had stopped in, though. So with the lack of customers or busywork, Davy had time to realize that in just a couple of weeks, he'd actually grown accustomed to having people around—other than his worrywart uncle. Who'd've thunk it? Which made not seeing any of them after such a long, boring day a major bummer, and he wasn't ashamed to admit it.

Finally, 9:00 p.m. rolled around, and after taking out what little trash had accumulated throughout the day and taking care of the few closing duties he hadn't already finished, Davy turned out the lights and locked the shop up for the night. He was happy to find that the night air was still warm, only a cool breeze from the Pacific reminding him that it wasn't quite summer yet. The streets were deserted, aside from a few homeless people camped out under the pavilion in the park.

As he stood waiting for the crosswalk signal to tell him he could walk, a familiar car approached. The blue Mitsubishi stopped abruptly at the curb beside him and rolled its window down. Davy leaned down to see Sean leaning across the center console with his usual friendly smile. "How much you charge for the *full monty*?"

Davy smiled. "You could never afford it." He wasn't sure at what point he'd developed the ability to joke about sex with Sean. He sure as hell couldn't with Gavin. Gavin mentioning sex still made Davy's insides turn to mush and his face turn a bright shade of red.

"I'm glad I caught you. A few of us are headed out to the beach. It's nothing fancy, but it's a brown-bag beach and we'll have a bonfire."

"Brown-bag beach?"

Sean's look was incredulous. "Dude. You're so lucky you met me."

Davy snorted. "The jury's still out on that one."

Sean threw his middle finger up. "Brown-bag beaches let you have liquor as long as they're in a brown paper bag. Pretty self-explanatory." Sean waved a brown bag that had a bottle of something in it. "Wanna party?"

Davy felt the familiar butterflies in his stomach telling him it was probably a really bad idea.

"I know, I know, you don't like the crowds, but you know once we get some booze in you you'll totally enjoy yourself. We're just chilling and it's the *beach*, hombre."

"Isn't hombre a Mexican thing?"

"Shut the fuck up and get in the car, Davy." Sean pushed open the passenger-side door.

Against his better judgment, Davy slid into the passenger seat, all knees and elbows. At five foot eleven, he wasn't terribly tall, but the car was definitely more suited for Sean's five-foot-seven stature.

They drove for about twenty minutes talking about nothing in particular. Traffic was light on the freeway and over the bridge to West Seattle. Davy loved the view of the cityscape from the other side of the bay. He rarely wandered farther than his apartment in Queen Anne, so he didn't get the view of the Space Needle and tall buildings with their blue-tinted glow very often.

When they arrived at the beach, Sean parallel-parked on the oceanfront road and announced they'd made it. Davy had to hold back a caustic *no shit*, because he could plainly see a bonfire with about twenty people his age gathered around. He'd never been to anything like this. *Shocker.* It seemed more suited for high schoolers, but he wouldn't say that to Sean.

"Hey, take a shot of this." Sean held out the open bottle of liquor he'd just taken a sip from. "And stop freaking out."

"I'm not freaking out." Davy knew he sounded like a two-year-old, and it hadn't convinced Sean if the patronizing look he shot him was anything to go by. "Fine," Davy said as he snatched the bottle. "What is it?"

"It's just vodka. Here. Chase with this." Sean offered him a can of Red Bull. Davy scrunched up his nose. Red Bull was certainly not his favorite, but it was better than nothing. He took a long drink from the bottle, and Sean laughed at him as he chugged the Red Bull to soothe the burn the liquor left in his throat.

"Gah! What the hell? Did you buy the cheapest crap they had?" Davy opened his door and spat on the ground to get some of the bitterness out of his mouth.

"Of course. It's about the buzz, not the taste." Sean said this as if he were sharing the meaning of life.

41

"Spoken like a true alcoholic."

"Spoken like a true smart-ass. I think I miss the quiet Davy. You've become so fresh lately." Sean gave him a lighthearted shove. That made Davy clam up again, but he smiled brighter than usual, feeling the booze soothe his nerves. This was why he didn't drink often. The liquid courage was addicting, and the last thing he needed was to become dependent because that less-inhibited feeling was a joyous thing.

He followed Sean out of the vehicle and shivered as the cool breeze nipped around him. "Heads up!" He turned just in time to catch a hoodie Sean had thrown him. He mumbled a thanks that probably went unheard over the wind blowing off the sound. It also would have helped if he hadn't said it while pulling the hoodie over his head. Sean handed Davy the vodka and can of Red Bull, then led the way, carrying blankets.

Sean called out their arrival to everyone. Mason and Devon approached with fist bumps and hellos and took blankets from Sean to spread on the sand. Nate, as usual, stood back with a hesitant welcome. Davy wondered again what the guy's problem was. He noticed quickly that Gavin was missing among the group of people gathered around the bonfire. He was disappointed but didn't have time to think on that feeling too long. Sean snagged him by the arm and led Davy over to the group for introductions. He was glad Sean had left him in charge of the booze so he could take a couple more pulls from the bottle. Soon, Sean noticed his discomfiture. He assured Davy he'd socialized enough that no one would think him rude if he went and relaxed where they'd spread the blankets. And that was exactly what Davy did.

Someone eventually opened a car door and turned up the radio. Everyone started dancing together. It didn't take long before most of them were drunk, some wasted. Davy sipped from the bottle every once in a while, enjoying the starry night and the sloshing of the water that could be heard over the music. He'd always preferred being the fly on the wall, anyway. He was amused at the antics of the other people.

He'd been distracted by Sean and Mason doing a slow grind against each other, wondering if something was there, when he became acutely aware of someone standing beside him. He knew who it was before he even looked up. He could *feel* Gavin's presence. Gavin was watching the action too. He gave Davy a pat on the shoulder, then eased down to sit beside him. He looked comfortable in a gray hoodie and khaki shorts. Davy wanted so badly to wrap his arms around Gavin and sit there for hours. He knew he'd said *just friends*, but sometimes it was impossible to ignore how strong his attraction to Gavin was. He trusted Gavin as a friend more and more every day, but he knew how Gavin operated in the romance department. Davy had been burned enough to know not to even touch a guy like Gavin. Gavin seemed to have lost interest anyway. Not that Davy could blame him after he'd been such a freak.

Nothing brings the boys to the yard like a hot mess. He laughed at himself derisively.

"What are you laughing at?" Gavin bumped Davy's shoulder with his own.

"Nothing," Davy mumbled. "Must be the booze."

"Right." Gavin always sounded as if he knew Davy better than Davy knew himself, and it annoyed the hell out of Davy. Gavin pulled a flask out of the pocket of his hoodie. "Whiskey?"

Davy studied the flask. "Really? You carry a flask? Who does that?"

"Hey! Don't hate. This flask has saved me from paying for expensive drinks in clubs many a time."

Davy rolled his eyes. "Classy."

"Always." Gavin patted Davy's back, eyes dancing jovially. Davy felt the touch down to his toes and was annoyed at how quickly his cock responded. It didn't help that Gavin smelled delicious. Normally the smell of cigarette smoke would piss him off and Gavin definitely smelled of that, but he also smelled like cologne. Davy never would have imagined cigarettes and Polo would be a turn-on.

They sat silently for a few moments. Davy couldn't seem to find his voice, but for once he didn't feel the need. He soaked in the comfort of having Gavin close. He wondered if Gavin felt the strange peace that existed between them too. *Not likely. You told him to get lost, remember?*

"Wanna—"

"How was—"

They started to speak and laughed when they stopped. Davy put his hand over his mouth. "Sorry. Go ahead."

Gavin studied him for a minute. Damn the man for always making him burn deep in his soul with just a look. "Wanna stop being a wallflower and dance?"

Davy shook his head and didn't miss a beat with his vehement "No. No, thanks."

Gavin nodded once. "Cool. Well, I'm gonna go say hey to everyone."

Davy didn't respond, just returned to his people watching. Gavin used Davy's shoulder to push himself up, then walked down to the group of dancing bodies, who all stopped to greet him. Davy was envious of Gavin's confidence. Gavin seemed to travel on another plane, and it made everyone gravitate toward him. Davy couldn't be more different if he tried. No wonder Gavin was okay with being just friends. And Davy couldn't figure out why that bothered him so much. Not like he dated. Dating was too messy. And Lord knew Gavin didn't date. He was like a tomcat. He prowled and took what he wanted, and then he'd slink away in the morning to go find someone else to feed him. Davy was intrigued while at the same time being put off by that fact. If he didn't know Gavin was more than a total player, he'd never consider him friend material.

Davy watched them all in wonder for a few minutes, then decided he'd had enough booze for the night, so he wandered back to Sean's car to get the bottled water from the messenger bag he'd left in the backseat. He returned to the blanket, but before he settled back down in his spot, he caught a glimpse of Gavin, whose body was plastered to a larger guy, mouths sensuously close to kissing as they slid against each other to the beat of the music. It was hot, but it made Davy's stomach clench with jealousy. He couldn't call it anything but jealousy. He wanted to hurl up all the alcohol he'd consumed. He knew he had no right to feel this way, but he couldn't stop the emotion from becoming overwhelming.

Then they kissed. Davy turned abruptly to leave but was caught by Nate.

"Davy, where ya headed?"

Of course Nate would decide to talk to him *now*. "Uh, I'm gonna go catch the bus. I have to be up early, and I don't wanna drag anybody away."

Nate gave him a funny look. "It'll take forever to get back by bus. Are you sure you don't wanna wait?"

Davy knew Nate was right. He weighed his options for a moment, but when he looked over to see Gavin and the guy he'd been dancing with walking off hand-in-hand to a darker part of the beach, Davy smacked himself mentally. "Nah. I'm just gonna head out. Tell Sean I said thanks for inviting me."

Davy could see that Nate had seen exactly why Davy was leaving.

"Typical," Nate grumbled, as if maybe his statement was a bit more personal than Davy knew. Of course it would be. The rich kid would be right up Gavin's alley. Nate was pretty in a yacht-club kind of way. Perfectly cut brown hair, bright-green eyes, polos and khaki shorts no matter where they went. He was tan from his mocha hair down to his blue Sperrys. Suddenly, Davy *really* needed to get the hell out of there.

"Have a good night, Nate."

He didn't wait for a response before slipping off down the street, never happier to hear anything other than the fading voices signaling he was getting far away from that party. Far away from Gavin.

CHAPTER SEVEN

GAVIN WAS good and annoyed as he stood in line at a hot-dog stand on Pine waiting to order his lunch. He thought he'd gotten somewhere with Davy. He thought they'd at least developed a decent friendship, but over the past week, Davy had started freezing him out again. He'd seemed fine at the party, but after that night, any time Gavin went into Bart's alone, Davy's face shuttered and his smiles were forced. Gavin found himself thinking *what the fuck?* quite often. He didn't get it. He'd gotten to the point that he'd stopped going in altogether by the time another week of Davy's freaky behavior had passed. Sean said they'd had lunch a couple of times, but they never talked about Gavin. Sean said he could sense something wrong too, though, so it wasn't just Gavin's imagination.

He hated to think it, but it'd be nice to have Davy's quiet presence around him. Gavin felt an eerie sense of calm when he was with Davy. He didn't understand it, but he needed it. That scared him, but right now he'd take what he could get.

He couldn't remember if he'd mentioned Ray's cancer in any of his conversations with Davy, but the oncologist had found out the radiation hadn't helped. Ray was going to die. Gavin was going to be alone. Again. And damn if Davy wasn't who he wanted to talk to. Damn if he knew why. The guys had been sympathetic enough, but they couldn't understand it. They all still had their families. Yeah, his mom was still around, but she could rot for all he cared. Ray was who he had, and soon he would be gone. No one would understand that like Davy, who spoke reverently about his mother. She'd fucked him up with her overbearing nature and fears of the world, but in the end she'd been Davy's person. His comfort. Davy would know what it was like to lose that.

Gavin couldn't get through this as he did other things. He couldn't drink and go out with the boys and hook up with random guys and expect everything to be better in the morning. That was impossible. He'd have to sleep through half of Seattle to numb himself to this. He hadn't even had it in him to do more than make out with the guy at the party. The guy had tried for more, but Gavin left him with his number and an apology, blaming it on whiskey dick.

He was not himself and he knew it. He didn't want to dump this on Ray either. He was trying to put on a brave face. If Ray could be brave about dying, then Gavin could be brave about seeing him through to the end. Ray deserved that. Not like his piece-of-shit daughter would drag her sorry ass around to help out.

Gavin couldn't let himself think about his mother right now, though. Thinking about Carmen Walker would make him officially lose his shit, and he didn't have time. He had Ray, and a friendship that had become important to him all quickly slipping away at the same time. He had to get his head in the game.

He remembered he needed to call Nate. Sean said Nate had talked to Davy before he left. Nate was the one who told Sean Davy'd taken the bus. Gavin remembered how disappointed he'd been when he ditched the guy on the beach and just wanted five more minutes of silent comfort from Davy, only to find he'd gone. He was surprised Davy hadn't even tried to find him to say good-bye. It was all so confusing.

His turn finally came up and he placed his order. While he waited for the vendor to top his brat with cream cheese and grilled onions, he dialed Nate's cell. He'd been avoiding it until the last minute. Nate had been weird lately too, so he'd hoped Davy would come around before he had to call in Nate's assistance. Nate answered right as the vendor handed Gavin his bratwurst in exchange for a ten-dollar bill, keep the change.

"Nate-dawg, what's up?"

"Oh. Hey, Gavin. How's it going?"

"I asked first." He stared longingly at his lunch and prayed Nate wouldn't drag this on in the bitchy way he tended to do when Gavin needed something.

"I'm good. We're at the yacht club down in Tacoma."

Gavin rolled his eyes. One reason he'd never be very close to Nate was the guy's pompous way of mentioning his family's money all the time. Gavin didn't think it was consciously done, but that almost made it worse. Gavin knew his family wasn't hurting for anything thanks to his gramps investing well and money from his grandmother's side of the family. In fact, Gavin's trust fund probably looked better than Nate's. He just didn't spend his like Nate did. He'd take Vans and American Eagle jeans any day. But Nate, Nate only wore Ralph Lauren and the like. It was obnoxious. But he wasn't all bad, so Gavin hoped he could appeal to his softer side today.

"That's cool." Gavin walked back to his truck and jumped in, then laid his lunch on the armrest. "So, I have a question." He could have sworn he heard an unpleasant "Of course you do," but he chose to ignore it. "So you saw Davy before he left the party the other night, right?"

"Yes, Gavin. What about it?"

Gavin pulled the phone back and looked at it for a second. *Rude, much?* "Did he seem okay? He's been weird lately, and I wondered if somebody had said something to him or something."

Nate huffed into the phone. Gavin was beginning to wonder if there was some secret We Hate Gavin Club meeting behind his back. He wouldn't be surprised with Nate, though. They'd had a couple run-ins over Nate's one-sided crush on Gavin. Gavin had never even pretended there was a hope for any kind of relationship with Nate, or anyone, for that matter. He figured his obvious concern for Davy was probably rubbing Nate the wrong way, but he didn't know what he could do about it. After a minute listening to shuffling and some muffled speaking on the other end of the line, Nate finally came back.

"Dude, why haven't you tried, I don't know, asking *him*?"

"Because that'd only get me so far with him. Dude, you know he's not one to talk about his problems."

Nate huffed again. Gavin considered throwing his phone but that wouldn't make him feel any better and wouldn't get him any closer to whatever Nate knew. "Nate, c'mon. Did he say anything weird before he left?"

"Look, Gavin. All I know is he looked pretty crushed when you walked off to hook up with that dude at the party. I'd almost talked him into staying or at least waiting for a ride until he saw you guys wander off."

Gavin grimaced. How'd he not even consider that?

"I thought you guys were just friends, anyway." *Oh yeah. That's why.*

"We are. I don't know why it'd bother him."

"Well it did. Bad. Are we done here?"

"Yeah. Sure. Thanks a lot, Nate."

Nate didn't hear the thanks, though. He'd already ended the call. Gavin didn't have the energy to deal with that now. He was too busy reeling from the idea that Davy may have actually been interested in him, and he may have fucked it up, yet again. He could handle Davy not wanting him and being his friend, but he couldn't handle not having Davy around at all because they were both suffering from what they thought were unrequited feelings. He was horrified to try anything, though. He wasn't exactly relationship material, and they were about as compatible in that department as oil and water. All he knew was that he needed to tread carefully if he didn't want to lose Davy for good. And for some reason, he knew he couldn't handle that.

GAVIN TOOK a deep breath and held his fist up to knock. Davy was on the other side of that door, and everything in Gavin was being pulled toward the man. He didn't understand it—the need that made his stomach cramp with nerves. It was that feeling that made him want to turn and run the other way, leaving Davy to think the worst of him so they could fade out of each other's lives. But even the thought of that made Gavin's heart thud with misery.

He'd driven around for twenty minutes before deciding to drive over to Davy's apartment. In the end, something in his gut wouldn't let him not go. So he'd made the trip up to Davy's door on the fourth floor, where he'd paced the halls after his first two aborted attempts to knock on the door.

He'd never chased after someone, certainly not a friend. He didn't feel the need to explain himself to anyone, but the idea that he'd hurt Davy didn't sit well with him. He didn't have a damn clue what to say, though. Charm would never work on Davy. The guy seemed immune to all of Gavin's usual tricks.

Man up, loser. He took a deep breath and finally knocked. He waited for a moment and heard no movement on the other side of the door. He considered knocking again, then considered leaving. Davy might not even be home. Hell, Gavin could have had the wrong apartment. He'd only dropped Davy off once or twice but he'd never been inside. He'd had to look at the mailboxes in the lobby for Cooper and hoped he had the right one.

When the door cracked open, Gavin exhaled in relief as Davy's familiar blue eyes blinked through the opening and he swung the door wider. "Gavin? What are you doing here?"

Gavin held up a six-pack. "I come bearing gifts."

Davy looked mildly put out. "You guys are seriously trying to give me a drinking problem."

Gavin shrugged. "What can I say? We like to share the love." Davy's face went stone-solid at that, making Gavin wince. "Bad choice of words." Davy stared. "Can I come in?"

Davy looked as though he wanted to say no, but manners obviously won over agitation and he opened the door all the way, gesturing with a sweep of his hand for Gavin to enter.

Gavin wandered in, taking in his surroundings. The studio was simple. A daybed that doubled as a couch sat against one wall. An entertainment center and coffee table were the only other furniture. There was nothing on the walls. It felt more like a hotel room than an apartment. Gavin imagined there were jail cells with more personality.

Davy gathered notebooks and his laptop up off the couch. "Here. Have a seat." After placing his burden on the coffee table, Davy wandered into the small kitchen that took up half of the floor space and retrieved a glass. "Do you want a glass for your beer?" He was still distant, but the hospitable offer gave Gavin a small seed of hope.

"You pour your beer in a glass?" Gavin teased. Davy scowled. Okay, no teasing. "No thanks." He set the six-pack down next to the couch and handed a beer over to Davy before taking a seat.

Davy just looked down at it for a moment. He set it on the kitchen counter, then turned to Gavin with a wariness in his eyes that made Gavin want to weep.

"What do you want, Gavin?"

And wasn't that the million-dollar question? "I guess the better question is what do *you* want, Davy?"

"What does that mean?"

Defensive. Great.

Gavin held his hands up in front of him. "Hey, I don't mean anything by it, Davy." Davy crossed his arms over his chest and looked down at his feet. "I thought we were cool, though—friends, even. But Nate tells me you got upset that I was hanging out with that guy at the beach."

Davy scowled at his feet, then met Gavin's eyes defiantly. "Maybe I just think you're better than that. Guess I'm just naïve."

The admission made Gavin's heart flutter. Was Davy saying that he cared, or was it just a friend wanting better for a friend? And why in the hell did Gavin want it to be the former so badly?

"That means a lot, Davy." Davy scoffed and Gavin jumped up and crossed the room to Davy. Both hands on Davy's shoulders, looking into soulful blue eyes that widened a bit at the closeness, Gavin said, "Honestly. It does. Mean a helluva lot."

Davy's gaze never wavered. That intense appraisal was unnerving. It seemed uncharacteristic of Davy. He seemed to have found something he didn't want to back down from. If only he'd—

Davy swooped in and claimed Gavin's mouth in a fierce kiss. *Holy wow!* The move was… unexpected. But damn were those pillowy lips warm and inviting. Gavin refused to pass up this moment of insanity Davy was suffering from. He wrapped his hand around Davy's neck and carded his fingers through Davy's soft hair. Davy grasped at Gavin's shirt and pulled him closer. Davy was breathing heavily as he opened his mouth to Gavin's seeking tongue. When their tongues met, Gavin sighed. Davy tasted like peppermints and something undeniably male. Gavin's whole body responded to the slide of their tongues. They were both grunting as they pressed their hips together and rocked into each other, cocks straining against fabric. Davy made such erotic mewling sounds in the back of his throat. Those sounds were enough to make Gavin weak in the knees.

As quickly as he'd started the kiss, Davy pulled back. He seemed as shocked at his actions as Gavin. Gavin didn't want him to stop. Ever.

"Davy?" Gavin's voice was rough to his own ears. Davy's lips looked damn good swollen from kissing. Davy placed his palm against Gavin's face and ran his thumb over Gavin's bottom lip. A shudder ran through Gavin's body and his cock ached for some skin. *Davy's skin, please!*

Watching the emotions play over Davy's face was confusing. Gavin wasn't sure whether he should step back and give the guy space or not. Much as he didn't want to, it was Davy's call. "Davy? What are we doing?" Fuck. His voice was shaking.

The question seemed to make up Davy's mind. He didn't speak and moved back in for another breathtaking kiss.

CHAPTER EIGHT

DAVY WASN'T exactly sure what in the hell had come over him. He'd felt such a strong urge to claim Gavin. The thought of Gavin continuously giving himself to other people when Davy was right here threatened to eat him alive. It was horrifying and he knew he should be totally mortified at his actions, but fuck if he could make himself give a shit in that moment.

He'd almost not answered the door earlier. He never had guests, so he honestly thought the knock had been on someone else's door. Something in him felt Gavin's presence, though. He wasn't sure why he'd developed a sixth sense where Gavin was concerned. He tried so hard to ignore it. He didn't want Gavin coming into his apartment. He didn't want Gavin's beer. He wanted to just be angry and for Gavin to go away.

Why did he keep showing up? And why couldn't Davy ignore him?

That shaking voice, Gavin's fight to restrain himself for Davy's sake, had sealed the deal. No way could he deny it anymore. He wanted Gavin. *Wanted* him. Wanting Gavin was stupid. Getting involved with him was reckless. He acted like the idiots who had fucked Davy over on the rare occasions he'd given in to the need to try the dating thing. He had no faith being with Gavin would end any better, and he didn't want to lose Gavin as a friend, but he couldn't deny that the last week had been hell. And he needed that kiss. He melted with that kiss.

Davy put both of his hands on Gavin's smooth face as their tongues danced together. It was probably the best kiss Davy ever had. The things

Gavin could do with his mouth were mind-numbing. Their mouths together were hot, wet, and demanding. They fought a battle for dominance, but Davy eventually gave in to Gavin's wicked probing tongue. His head was swimming from the smell of Gavin's cigarettes and cologne. He felt high.

Davy pulled back again only because his lungs were screaming for air. Gavin rested his forehead on Davy's and fought for air himself. Davy closed his eyes, enjoying the feeling of Gavin's fingers running through the hair on the back of his head. The moment felt so heavy. *This is just sex for Gavin. Don't get emotionally involved.* The thought almost cooled his desire, but Davy couldn't stop what he was doing. He could do sex, just this once. He knew sex complicated things, but since he was going into this eyes wide open, maybe he wouldn't be setting himself up to get hurt like in the past. Gavin wasn't promising him anything other than that right now, unlike those other guys in Davy's past.

He knew Gavin was trouble. Big trouble. He was shocked to realize he was totally okay with that. Even more than his brain, his cock was definitely okay with the idea of getting it on with Gavin. Who wouldn't want to? The guy's every pore exuded bad-boy sex appeal.

"You okay?" Davy almost missed Gavin's throaty whispered question. Knowing Davy was the one who had Gavin so lust-stricken zinged right down into Davy's balls.

"Never better," Davy said as he pushed Gavin toward the couch, then captured those full lips with his own. There was no finesse, just clinking teeth and sexy grunts. They tumbled onto the couch in a writhing mess of limbs and roaming hands. Gavin was so firm. Davy could rub against the man like a cat and purr for hours.

Davy sat up and they helped each other strip off shirts. Gavin's hands on Davy's chest sent electricity up his spine. He closed his eyes and moaned when Gavin pinched his nipples.

"So sexy, Davy." Gavin's voice was an octave deeper than usual, heavy with lust.

Davy looked into half-lidded eyes and saw heat there. He couldn't believe that heat was for him. He'd seen the guys Gavin had hooked up with and he didn't feel he fit in that league. He didn't know what the hell

Gavin saw in him, but he didn't give a shit about that when Gavin rocked his hips into Davy's. Their cocks mashed together through denim.

Gavin closed his eyes as he continued rolling his hips against Davy's. Davy took a minute to appreciate Gavin's bare torso. He had a strong chest with a smattering of hair and a few tattoos, a smooth, flat stomach, and a perfect *V* leading to the treasure in his pants. Davy leaned down to place a peck on Gavin's lips, using his hands to still Gavin's hips so he could slowly lick the lines of each tattoo. He started with the ink on Gavin's chest, then worked his way to each of the many on Gavin's arms. By the time Davy got to the single anchor tattoo on Gavin's hipbone, Gavin was putty in his hands, writhing and panting.

Davy smiled as he scraped his teeth gently over Gavin's hipbone. Gavin watched him through his long eyelashes, mouth hanging open. Davy almost shot his load in his pants just from the expression on Gavin's face. Davy was too far gone to back down now. He kissed Gavin's anchor tattoo again as he eased the zipper on Gavin's jeans open. Gavin stilled his hand.

"Are you sure about this, Davy?"

The fact Gavin stopped him to ask that question made any doubts Davy might have had fly right out of his head. Not that he'd been concentrating on much more than praying at the temple that was Gavin's body. He popped the button to Gavin's jeans—*holy fuck, commando!*—and wrapped his fingers around Gavin's cock in answer.

Gavin's head fell back. "Fuuuuuck, Davy."

Gavin lifted his hips off the couch, assisting Davy's attempt to pull Gavin's pants down enough to get at his cock. Gavin's hard cock rose long, graceful, and proud. Gavin's cut cock was bigger than Davy had imagined. Not incredibly long, but longer than average and thick. There was a bead of precum forming at the slit that Davy couldn't resist spreading with his thumb. Gavin gasped as Davy took the warm length of him in hand and stroked with a firm grip, concentrating on a steady twisting over the head.

Gavin's body went rigid. "Davy, baby. You gotta stop. I'm gonna blow."

Davy eased up. He was definitely not finished with that cock. It had been way too long since he'd last been this close to one, and this was the most beautiful cock he'd ever seen. This was a porn-star cock, and he wanted to enjoy it while it was his to enjoy.

He gave Gavin his best wicked grin, unsure what the hell had come over him. *Hormones are a helluva thing.* He shifted on his knees, moving between Gavin's legs, gripped the base of Gavin's cock, and swirled his tongue around the head.

"Gahhhhhh!" Gavin groaned.

Davy reveled in the salty taste of his essence. He closed his lips around the head and made a slow descent. Gavin put his hand on the back of Davy's head. He didn't force him, just touched. The look of awe playing across his face made Davy determined to make this awesome for him. He started a steady rhythm up and down with his mouth and his hand, sucking hard, massaging with his tongue. Gavin was too thick to go down Davy's throat, but Davy could take him in until the tip of his cock touched the back of Davy's throat.

He pulled off the cock and continued stroking, using his spit to slick the way. He eased down to Gavin's balls, inhaling the strong scent of his musk. Nothing felt more intimate that knowing these parts of him. Davy tried to file away every image, every sight, every smell. He sucked in one ball, earning a hiss from Gavin, then the other. He flicked his tongue in circles around Gavin's sac. Gavin's knuckles went white as they clutched the couch.

Davy took him back into his mouth and encouraged Gavin to thrust. Gavin let loose steady thrusts with *fucks* and *so goods*. Gavin's responses had Davy so hard he thought his cock might break. He reached into his pants, took himself in hand, and stroked. He kept a strong suction and a firm grip on Gavin, and Gavin took what was offered.

"Fuck. Fuck, fuck, fuck. Davy. Baby, I'm gonna come."

Davy didn't let up, even as Gavin's body tensed and he groaned from somewhere deep inside his guts. Davy decided to bite the bullet, knew his throat would be sore for a week, but he swallowed Gavin's thick length, freeing up his hand to roll Gavin's balls in their sac. That did Gavin in.

"*Shiiiiiiiit!*" Gavin rolled forward, toward the orgasm, clutching Davy's shoulders.

Gavin's release shot down Davy's throat, and he moaned. He had never been so eager to take another person's load before. Watching Gavin come completely undone was a thing of fucking beauty.

Davy eased off Gavin's cock and licked it clean. Gavin worked on catching his breath for a moment, then reached down to pull Davy up for a sloppy kiss. "Damn, Davy. I taste good in your mouth." Gavin pecked Davy's nose, then his eyelids, then his lips. Gavin shifted so he could reach into his pocket, then pulled out a condom. Davy eyed it carefully. Yeah, he'd totally let him—

Gavin held it out to him.

"What am I doing with this?"

Gavin laughed at him. "What do you think? You're gonna fuck me."

Davy reared back. "Uh, I'm pretty exclusively a bottom."

Gavin's eyes went wide. He slid from under Davy and moved into sitting position. "A bottom?" Davy nodded, not getting where this was going until—wait. *Shit.*

"Shit. You too, huh?"

Gavin looked as though someone had kicked his puppy. "Yeah. I've never been a huge fan of being on top." He started setting himself to rights and Davy eyed him warily.

"So what does that mean?"

Gavin ran his hands over his face, then stood and buttoned his jeans. "Well, it means us and sex are incompatible. You got a wicked mouth on you, man. But, uh, this was obviously a mistake."

Davy felt as though he'd been sucker-punched. His hard-on immediately deflated as he realized he was about to be ditched. "Are you shitting me?" he asked.

Gavin didn't even acknowledge him as he slid his shirt on. "Well, at least we got that out of our systems."

"Seriously? You're leaving?" Davy pulled a blanket from under the couch and covered himself, suddenly feeling very dirty, used.

"Yeah. I got shit to do." Gavin gathered up his keys and his cell phone from the coffee table and headed toward the door. He never looked back even as he gave a halfhearted "See ya around."

When the door clicked shut behind him, Davy could only sit and stare. He knew Gavin was an asshole and he'd prepared himself. But that didn't stop the sob that tore from his throat. He didn't know why it hurt more when Gavin did this, but he knew he never wanted to see that son of a bitch again.

CHAPTER NINE

GAVIN LOOKED at the time on his phone for what must be the millionth time. He really didn't have the patience for Macroeconomics this morning, and class hadn't even started. He'd almost missed all the allotted days for absences for the current quarter carting Ray around to doctor appointments. Not that that'd be a problem anymore. But he couldn't think about that. Not that his brain let him think about anything other than Ray's prognosis.

Oh, and don't forget about Davy. His brain had fun taunting him like that a lot these days.

Gavin knew he'd really fucked up with Davy. Sure, he'd freaked out, but he'd never fucking ditched out on a guy like that before. It definitely wouldn't be the first time he'd ended up in a two-bottoms situation. Usually that was solved by bringing in a third or some hot sixty-nine action. Somehow he didn't imagine the former would have been cool with Davy. Although, even joking about it would have been better than being ditched and blue-balled. Gavin would have kicked a guy's ass if he'd done that to him.

Fuck. Fuck, fuck, fuck. "I'm such an idiot."

"You? Noooo," Devon drawled as he slid into a seat beside him. They'd decided to take Macro together since Devon needed a lot of help and Gavin would breeze through it. Gavin's grades were so top-notch that his professor was fairly lenient about his absences.

"Dude, you calling me an idiot is pretty priceless," Gavin said. Devon's face was blank for a minute. He didn't easily pick up on sarcasm—or any joking for that matter that didn't involve such mature themes as penises or bodily functions. He was easily the prettiest of the group of friends, though, and completely unaware of it. He also had the biggest heart of anyone Gavin ever met. It was a bit shocking when you realized the depths beneath the ditziness.

Devon's face contorted after he'd thought on Gavin's words another moment. Gavin smiled when Devon finally retorted, "That was mean, G. You're not an idiot. You're an asshole."

Gavin laughed. "Down, boy." Devon balled up a piece of paper and threw it at him.

"Go *down on it*, boy," Devon said and waggled his eyebrows.

Gavin shook his head. "You're hopeless." He threw the paper ball back at Devon.

"Okay, there's still a while until class starts. Explain yourself. Why are you an idiot?"

Gavin hesitated. Devon wasn't usually the first person he'd go to for advice. Especially about a guy. Devon went through men like some people did clothes in a month. "It's nothing, really."

"Stop being dumb. We can all tell something is up with Davy, and you've been weird the last few days, so I'd be willing to bet you did something to the guy."

"Why do you automatically assume it was me that did something?" Gavin protested.

Devon's *oh please* expression was flawless. It stopped Gavin from further feigning his innocence. "Okay. You're right. But I really don't want to talk about it."

"One of you is going to have to talk about it soon because it's all weird. Not like Davy is our bestie, but he's pretty cool and I don't want to feel like a jerk just because I want to stop in for a Twinkie shake. And you know that guy is the only one who makes 'em right."

"Seriously? This is about you wanting your Twinkie-shake fix?"

"You bet your sweet ass, G-man." Devon smirked unapologetically. "If you get between me and my shake dealer, I promise he will win."

Gavin laughed. "Again. You're hopeless."

"We've established that. I'm a hopeless idiot; you're a feminine hygiene product and the bag it came in. So can we move on to what you did to convince *Davy* of that fact?"

Gavin sighed. *May as well.* "Well, we kinda hooked up—"

"Dude, shut up! He let *you* deflower him?"

"Shut the fuck up. He was not a virgin. Do you wanna hear this or not?"

Devon did the lock-and-key gesture over his mouth but still looked completely surprised. "So, we hooked up. Only when we were moving on to the main event it turned out that we were both, er, bottoms."

"Ouch," Devon said earnestly. "So what'd you do?"

"Well, I kinda freaked out. I spazzed and left him holding his own cock."

Gavin reared back at the sudden "*What? Are you the biggest dick ever?*" that erupted from his friend. Gavin was sure people turned to stare at them, but since that was nothing new for them, he didn't pay any attention.

"I told you. I fucked up. So I don't blame him for being upset."

"Well, did you talk to him about it? Explain yourself?"

"I didn't really know why I reacted that way. And I've kind of ignored his texts because I don't know what the hell to say."

Devon sat staring at him, wide-eyed in shock. He opened his mouth a few times to say something but never spoke. Gavin squirmed under his gaze. Yeah, Devon was the best of them. So it really smarted knowing he was *actually* being thought of as an asshole. But he knew he totally deserved it, no matter how much it sucked. Davy had sent a few messages, even going so far as apologizing for some imagined infraction. That made Gavin feel like an even bigger tool, but he hadn't even shot Davy a simple *it's not you, it's me* to at least let him know he didn't do anything. Gavin was just a dumbass.

Before Devon got a chance to voice his opinions, the professor called the start of class. Gavin's mind returned to being miserable. He was pretty sure if he was honest with himself he'd know exactly why he'd freaked out on Davy, but he didn't want to be honest. Gavin's phone vibrated in his pocket. He glanced at Devon who had his phone in hand. He used to point it at Gavin's pocket, indicating he should check his own.

Gavin sighed and dug his phone out of his pocket and retrieved the text message. *U should say ur sorry. Prove that ur the good guy that I know U R.* Gavin looked up at Devon in surprise. It'd been a while since anyone said they thought he was a good guy. In fact, he couldn't remember if anyone had ever said it to him in his life. The idea of Gavin's mother or his high school boyfriend ever saying anything that nice to him made him snort. Devon gave Gavin a pointed glare, and Gavin knew he was right. He gave a nod, getting a pleased grin from Devon.

DAVY GRITTED his teeth when he saw that the person walking through the door to the shop was the last one he wanted to see. After three days of ignored messages, blown-off apologies, and a declined call, Gavin decided to show up in person? Davy *really* didn't have patience to deal with him. Fortunately there was a long line of customers. It'd be a while yet before they had to speak. Davy made sure to give his most withering glare to show Gavin he didn't appreciate him showing up unannounced. Gavin had the decency to look abashed and took a seat at the corner of the counter. He was out of the way, but Davy didn't want him there at all.

Davy had spent the last three days trying to figure out what he could have done wrong. He got that they were both bottoms and that was awkward, but that was no reason for Gavin to have treated him like total shit. Unless Davy *had* done something wrong. He'd run the emotional spectrum from mortification to anger to hurt the entire time until he'd admitted he'd, once again, fallen for the worst guy possible. He was lured in by the friendship, his lonely heart making him an easy target. Damn Gavin Walker.

And this is why you don't date, Davy. He needed to stop thinking about it because he was scowling at customers, even the regular blue-hair crowd who were obviously not sure how to respond to his obvious aggression as he banged around behind the counter. Davy noticed Gavin flinch a few times as he slammed something shut or placed a cup down harder than necessary. *Good, asshole. Now get the hint and fuck off.*

But Gavin didn't go away. He sat, waiting patiently, for about an hour as Davy finished up with customers and everyone eventually cleared out of the shop. Davy started cleaning up after he was sure he was finished with the rush, putting away ice cream and wiping the counters. He'd been doing such a good job of ignoring Gavin that he jumped when Gavin finally spoke.

"Can we talk?"

Davy turned to him with a scowl. "Go away, Gavin." He said it with as much ice in his tone as he could muster. Gavin's brown eyes held a hint of sadness. Dammit, Davy did not want to see that. Why couldn't Gavin just leave him alone?

"Davy, I know I'm an asshole."

"No shit." Davy turned away from him and started washing shake tins. He did not want to see things like the true regret in Gavin's face. This little game was getting old.

"I'm so sorry. I should never have done that to you. And I really shouldn't have ignored you afterward."

Davy grunted in response but refused to face him.

"Seriously, Davy. I know I keep fucking up with you. I do. I want to really explain myself, though. I'll sit here all day and wait for you to have coffee with me."

No way. Davy turned on Gavin, who reared back at whatever he saw in Davy's face. *Please don't let him see the hurt. Please, please, please.* "Go. Away." Davy leaned on the counter and got in Gavin's face. "I'm done with this crap. I don't have anything to say to you, Gavin."

Gavin held Davy's gaze, then softly placed his hands over Davy's where they lay on the counter. Davy really wanted to snatch them away, but he was hypnotized by the regret in Gavin's eyes.

Shit.

"Okay. I have a thirty-minute lunch coming up. That's all I'll give you."

Gavin perked up, smiling brightly. Davy was still angry enough he wanted to smack that grin off his face. Gavin could obviously sense the mutiny, because he put his hands up in surrender. "No pushing. Thank you. Thank you, thank you. I'll just run out and grab you something to eat. Taxi Dog? Falafel?"

Davy wouldn't look a gift horse in the mouth. *Or gift jackass in this case.* If he didn't have to leave to get food, then he'd actually get to sit down for thirty full minutes. "My feet thank you." Gavin quirked an eyebrow. "Can you go to the gyro place over—"

"On Pine. You like the chicken kabob, right?"

Davy confirmed, grudgingly. He didn't know how the hell Gavin would know that, but when it came to Gavin's mysterious ways, Davy had stopped asking questions.

Gavin's smile was brilliant as he waved and rushed out of the shop. Davy shook his head, unsure of what he was getting himself into. He didn't know if he could hold it together through another one of Gavin's colossal fuckups. He couldn't help thinking he'd be wise to lock the doors and pretend he'd left for lunch while Gavin was gone. But he knew he wouldn't. He was helpless where Gavin was concerned.

CHAPTER
TEN

GAVIN HELD his breath as he approached the soda shop. He knew Davy could very well have made a break for it after he'd sent Gavin off. It didn't seem like Davy's style, but Gavin wouldn't have blamed the guy, would have probably done it himself had the roles been reversed. When he got to the door and saw through the window that Davy was still waiting for him inside, he exhaled loudly.

The bells over the door sounded throughout the deserted shop as Gavin made his way in. Davy looked up from whatever he was doing, a ghost of a smile barely lifting the corners of his mouth. Gavin's heart stuttered with relief. Maybe that meant there was some hope here. All he needed was hope.

"Got the goods," Gavin said, holding up the bag of food and smiling. He tried to play it like he would any other day. Just act normal and let Davy loosen up around him, even if it was just a little. Davy came around the counter, put the *Gone to Lunch* sign up, and locked the door. Gavin sat down in one of the three booths at the back of the shop so they'd have privacy from anyone peeping through the windows. Davy took a seat across from him. Gavin passed over Davy's food, wondering at what point it might be appropriate to speak again. He felt so weird not just steamrolling through as he normally would, but the last thing Davy would accept today was Gavin being his usual heavy-handed and demanding self.

After taking a bite of his food, Davy finally glanced up at Gavin. "Well, let's hear it. You obviously want to say whatever it is bad enough.

I'm listening for"—Davy looked at his watch—"twenty minutes. That's all I've got time for."

Gavin tried to suppress a smile at Davy's attempt to be a hard-ass. The guy was too nice. He definitely had no trouble being annoyed, but Davy was anything but a hard-ass. *Cupcake, more like it.* Gavin took a bite of his own lunch to muffle the snort that thought caused. Davy cocked his head in question, clearly unamused.

Gavin cleared his throat and put his food down, feeling about two inches tall. Great. "Um. Yeah. Sorry." He wiped his mouth with a napkin, buying a moment to gather his thoughts. Gavin could hear Devon in his head telling him not to fuck this up. "Okay, so I obviously owe you a huge apology." Davy snorted, and Gavin reached across to lay a hand on top of one of Davy's that he'd laid on the tabletop. Davy stilled, looking into Gavin's eyes. Gavin had never been so sincere when he said, "Honestly. I'm so sorry. Not just for freaking out, but for ditching you. You got me off and I left you sitting there. It was fucked-up and disrespectful."

Davy blushed and looked away, biting his bottom lip. Damn, but the guy was cute as hell. "D-did I do something?" Davy's gaze wandered everywhere but in Gavin's direction. Gavin's stomach clenched, guilt gnawing its way through him.

"Hey, you," Gavin said softly. "Look at me." A moment passed but Davy did eventually turn his gaze back. Gavin wanted to smother the guy with hugs. And damn if that wasn't a new one for him. Gavin Walker did *not* hug, much less did he think about *smothering* people with them. What was Davy doing to him?

"Davy, you didn't do anything. I'm an asshole. I had been trying so hard to get you to go out with me, even though I don't even date, and here I was getting in deeper than I figured I was capable. That's what freaked me out. I usually bottom, and when you said you did too, the fact that I didn't find that to be a big deal just made me flip out."

Davy looked confused. "Let me get this right. You freaked out because even though we are both bottoms, it wasn't a big deal?"

Gavin sighed and nodded. "I know it sounds crazy. It's just that I'm so used to it only being about sex—hard and fast—and when my brain realized I could do it slow and different with you, I realized that maybe I had real feelings for you."

Davy blinked. Blinked again. "But—"

"No buts." Gavin laughed. "Maybe literally." Davy rolled his eyes, bitching about what a stupid pun that was. "I just know it's not the only sex we could have, assuming we ever have sex again. And I want to have you around. And not just as a friend."

Davy chewed his lip again. "Gavin, I just don't know. You must realize how humiliating all of this has been."

Gavin gripped his hand tighter. "I know. I do know. I'm horrible. I'm a jerk and I just keep fucking up so bad where you're concerned, but if you could give me just one more chance, I want to show you I'm not all bad." Davy's eyes were clouded with doubt. "Don't say no. I'm begging." Gavin pointed to himself. "And Gavin Walker does *not* beg. Ever. So here I am, begging for you to just give me this one last chance."

Davy chewed it over for a minute. Gavin wanted to get up and pace, but he continued to sit, pleading with his eyes. Davy huffed an impatient breath. "I must be a glutton for punishment." Gavin's cheeks hurt from the force with which his smile stretched his face. Davy pointed at Gavin and continued, "Dude, this is your last time, though. I won't let you keep playing me."

Gavin was so pleased he couldn't do anything but jump up and rush Davy with a kiss. It wasn't heated, no tongues, just a quick press of their lips. He didn't pull back, though, until Davy relaxed and smiled against his lips. Gavin sat back, smiling at Davy. "I won't fuck it up." *At least I hope I won't*. Davy's face said he was thinking the same thing. "So I'm picking you up after work tonight. You've gotta meet someone."

Davy's eyes got a little wide. "M-meet someone?"

"I promise he won't bite." Gavin gave the Scout's-honor sign with his hand and started gathering his things. "Okay, I've got to jet." He stood up, still smiling like a fool, and planted another kiss on Davy's lips. He wasn't exactly sure what the hell had gotten into him, but he was diving into it headfirst, not that that was any different than any other time. Except this involved messy things like feelings. But he wouldn't dwell on that. "Pick you up after work!" Gavin didn't give Davy any time to respond or himself time to second-guess as he jetted out the door.

DAVY WASN'T sure what exactly Gavin had up his sleeve. In fact, he wasn't entirely sure what the hell he'd been thinking agreeing to get any further involved with Gavin. He figured his earlier assessment of being a glutton for punishment was pretty spot-on. Something in the sincerity Davy had seen in Gavin's eyes and heard in Gavin's words had touched him. And that smile Gavin had given him was enough to make a guy weak in the knees.

What was it someone had said about Gavin? Oh yeah. The boy was trouble. Gavin had proved that assessment true over and over again, but Davy just kept going back for more. It was those moments of vulnerability Gavin showed when he was around his friends, or when he was alone with Davy and had his I'm-too-cool-for-school swagger turned off. In those moments when Gavin's smile was genuine or when he looked at Davy as though maybe Davy had the answer to all his questions, Davy just couldn't help thinking Gavin was the most beautiful person he'd ever seen. Gavin's charm was unparalleled, but the moments where he was just Gavin were devastating. Davy hadn't been able to resist seeing him try to prove he wasn't a huge asshole. Maybe if he had more of Gavin being himself, Davy could run away with his heart. And wasn't that a scary fucking thought.

Davy finished his shift duties just around the time the new girl who worked night shift bounced in. She tried making conversation, but Davy couldn't keep up with her squirrelly chatter. He was tempted to see if throwing a shiny thing would make her run off in the other direction. Instead, he politely excused himself just in time for Gavin's huge truck to pull up in front of the shop. He made his way outside and hopped into the passenger seat, getting a quick peck on the lips from Gavin. Davy wasn't quite sure how to feel about Gavin's sudden penchant for stolen kisses.

"How was work?" Gavin asked.

Davy shot him an exasperated glance. "Really? 'How was work?'"

Gavin shrugged, looked hurt. "I was just trying to—"

"Trying too hard?" Davy wasn't sure where the sudden bitchiness came from. Gavin winced, put the truck into drive, and quietly pulled out onto the street. Davy was silent as they made their way back over the West Seattle Bridge. "Where are we going? Back to the beach?"

"No. It's boys' night at my house." Gavin sounded sullen.

Davy reached over and touched Gavin's arm that was resting on the armrest. "Sorry for being an ass, Gavin. It's hard for me to figure out how to act on a normal day in a normal situation. This is far from that."

"It's cool." Gavin didn't sound convinced, but he was smiling and shrugging all the same.

"No. That wasn't nice of me. I said I'd give you a chance." Davy wasn't sure what else to say, but everyone knew people were not his specialty.

As Gavin pulled off an exit and stopped at a red light, he took Davy's hand and squeezed. "No, you were right. I'm a bit nervous. I really don't want to fuck this up."

Davy was pleased to see Gavin was just as freaked out as he was. Gavin's nerves were refreshing. Davy squeezed his hand back and looked out the window as they drove down the road adjacent to Puget Sound. The view and the silence in the truck were comfortable. A baseball game played on low volume on the radio, and the sun hugged the islands in the horizon, threatening to make its final descent behind the trees, plunging the city into night. But it was early yet. Dark was a while away. The night was young, and Davy wondered what Gavin had planned.

His questions were answered as Gavin turned into a large house that sat across the street from the beach side of the road. There were a few classic cars in the driveway. Gavin patted Davy's knee. "Home sweet home."

Davy studied the Victorian home appreciatively. It was two floors and obviously older than the newer homes around it, but well cared for. "This is where you live?"

"Yep. This is my grandfather's house. He's been here for years. My mom was raised here." Gavin said the last part a bit begrudgingly.

"But you grew up in Maine?"

Gavin nodded, staring at the house. "My mom always said she couldn't get away from Seattle fast enough. Funny, I felt the same way about Rockland."

Davy wanted to ask more about Gavin's mom. It seemed to be a real sore subject, though, so he decided against it.

"All right. Let's go in. Fair warning: the guys are… rowdy."

Davy was going to ask what Gavin meant by that, but Gavin was already out of the truck and halfway to the front door. Davy jumped out and followed, coming up behind him right as Gavin opened the front door. Immediately, Davy scrunched his nose at the strong smell of cigar smoke. There was a thick layer floating around the ceiling light fixtures, making toxic halos. Gavin laughed and Davy realized it was at his disgusted expression.

"Yeah, they like their cigars on boys' night." Gavin took Davy by the hand. Davy wanted to protest but allowed Gavin to drag him along through a swinging door into a dining room with a large table surrounded by three elderly men, all laughing raucously. The room was stale with smoke, but the lights were bright and so were the smiles. There was an elderly lady sitting on one of the men's laps, and the table was covered in playing cards, poker chips, and tumblers of amber liquor that Davy assumed was whiskey. The room sure smelled like whiskey.

All heads turned toward them as they strolled in. Davy's eyes widened and his cheeks flushed at the sudden attention. The old woman jumped off the man's lap and bustled over to hug Gavin, who was smiling fondly as he bent to return her embrace one-armed since he refused to let go of Davy's hand. "Hey, Janie. Is Ray being fresh over there?"

"Always!" The old man whose lap Janie had been sitting in proclaimed, loud and proud.

Obviously that was the Ray Davy had heard so much about. He was definitely Gavin's grandfather. Davy could see the same gleam in their eyes and the same smirk on their mouths. He didn't look as sick as Davy had been led to believe.

"I thought he was dying or something."

Davy thought he whispered, but Ray responded, "He's dying, not deaf. And we call this going out with style."

Davy wanted the floor to open up and suck him in as all the others in the room laughed, even Gavin. *Traitor.* Gavin gave his hand a sympathetic squeeze. The Janie woman fussed over them both for a moment, short of squeezing Davy's cheeks. He was grateful she didn't go quite that far.

When Janie stepped away, Davy noticed that Ray was puffing on his cigar, sizing him up. "You done good with this one. He's pretty." The room erupted in laughter again. This time, even Gavin blushed. "Get him a drink, Gavin. He looks like he's gonna faint."

That was how the rest of the night went. The men picked on Davy and Gavin, they drank whiskey, and when Janie found out Davy's mother wasn't alive anymore she bustled around cooking because he was "too thin." It was well and late by the time the house cleared out. Davy couldn't remember having so much fun in a long time. He was sure the expensive whiskey had done the trick, but the company had been pretty amazing. They'd taken him in as one of their own. And Gavin—Gavin was like a different man. He was warm, obviously having a lot of respect and love for Ray and his friends. They all treated Gavin as though he was their own grandchild. Davy had made a joke about it being no wonder Gavin was so spoiled and gotten a wink, but no denial.

After midnight it was just Gavin and Ray playing a final round and Janie cleaning. She'd proven through the night there was nothing frail about her, despite her hunched shoulders and white hair. She was as much a character as Ray. Finally Gavin threw in his last card and turned a loose, happy grin on Davy. Davy's breath left his body briefly. Davy's heart stuttered, and he knew in that moment he was totally gone.

"So you're not a huge asshole all the time." Davy didn't know what made him say that. Something else he'd blame on the whiskey.

Gavin bumped Davy's shoulder with his own. "I'm glad you think so."

Davy rolled his eyes. "Way to play the gramps card, dude."

Ray laughed. "He learned from the best."

Davy shook his head. "I have no doubt."

Ray gave him a wink. Oh yeah. Gavin got all that old-school charm from Ray.

Gavin leaned over and kissed Davy's jaw. "Wanna come see my room?"

Davy's eyes threatened to pop out of his head. He couldn't believe Gavin had asked that in front of his grandfather, but Ray just rolled his eyes.

"You two go on." He waved them off. Davy died a little inside, but he didn't stop Gavin when he pulled him up and toward the door to the basement, waving a good-night to Janie who rolled her eyes much like Ray had. Yes. Davy was officially mortified. And he wasn't sure what the hell he was getting himself into.

CHAPTER ELEVEN

DAVY SHUFFLED from foot to foot as he took in Gavin's room while Gavin got beers from his refrigerator. Gavin's bedroom was actually a *few* rooms. The basement had been converted into a mother-in-law suite with its own bathroom, kitchenette, and small sitting room. There was a door that led outside so Gavin didn't have to use the front door at all unless he wanted.

Gavin's whole suite was bigger than Davy's studio. The suite was homier than Davy's apartment too. The walls were painted hunter green, and all the comfy-looking furniture was brown suede and plush. There were photos of Gavin and his friends framed and sitting on end tables. There were professional nature photographs on the walls, and on one wall a large flat-screen television that had a huge DVD collection on shelves underneath. If Davy had seen all of this a week earlier, he'd have thought it was nothing like Gavin, but Davy knew better now. Gavin was down-to-earth and comfortable. That was what his home said.

But comfortable was not the word Davy would use to describe the moment. Even with the whiskey still warming him, he wasn't sure how to act. He waited for Gavin to come back with the beers to figure out what to do. Gavin walked over to the couch and waved Davy over. Davy took a beer and slowly sat beside him. They drank in silence for a moment. Davy wanted so badly to have something to say, but he figured forcing conversation would be more awkward than the silence. And who knew?

Maybe it wasn't awkward silence. Gavin had his head leaned back, eyes closed with a serene smile on his face. And there went Davy's heart stuttering again.

When Gavin opened his eyes and caught Davy staring at him, the sudden heat in the brown depths made Davy swallow hard. Gavin's lips curled up into a playful grin, and Davy's treacherous cock lengthened in his pants. Gavin's gaze landed on the obvious bulge in Davy's shorts. The hunger on Gavin's face made Davy both nervous and impossibly hard. He couldn't tell whether his heart had stopped or whether it was just beating too fast to be heard.

Gavin reached for Davy's beer bottle and placed it, along with his own, on the coffee table. Without preamble he leaned in to suckle on Davy's jaw right behind the ear, hand caressing Davy's rigid cock. Davy made an inelegant squeak and struggled to catch his breath with the onslaught of feelings. Of course he was turned-on. Who wouldn't be? Gavin was ridiculously hot and smelled like whiskey and his expensive cologne. His lips were doing a number on the sensitive skin behind Davy's ear, his hand firmly coaxing Davy's cock into a tingling orgasm, even through Davy's shorts. That telltale itching sensation had begun to tingle Davy's balls.

Davy stilled Gavin's hand before he embarrassed himself. He struggled around heavy breaths to say, "Uh, Gavin, what are you doing?"

Gavin leaned back and leveled his gaze on him drily. And that damn grin. "I'd say I'm trying to get you off."

"Er. I thought we had a big issue in this department." Davy was not the best at talking sex, but he needed to know what Gavin was thinking. He wasn't sure he'd believed the lines Gavin had fed him earlier about the bedroom activities they could do. Surely Gavin didn't want to give up that part of sex since, judging by his reputation and the things Davy had seen with his own eyes, Gavin seemed so fond of sex.

"And I told you there's plenty of other stuff we can do. I meant it."

Davy averted his eyes. The sincerity in Gavin's expression scared him. "I can't handle it, Gavin. I can't handle falling for you to have you leave me because the sex isn't what you want. It's happened before. It's

74

always sex. They use it—sex. They fuck me over and I'm left with nothing because I was too quiet or too submissive or too boring."

Gavin took Davy's face in his hands and made Davy look at him. "That's not me, okay. I know I fucked up last time. I want to make that up. This is about you. And you aren't making me give up anything. Being with you felt so good. That's what I need. You. To touch you, feel you. The only rule to sex is that it's supposed to feel good to the people having it. There's no rules about *how* to have it as long as it makes the people involved feel close to each other."

Close to each other? Davy rolled his eyes. "I know that. But won't you—"

Gavin kissed him. It was soft and sensual. Those soft lips lit Davy on fire. He had so many more objections, but a gentle nibble to his bottom lip shut him up. Gavin positioned himself on top of Davy, lining their clothed cocks together and rolling his hips. Davy groaned. Gavin took advantage of Davy's parted lips, sinking his tongue into Davy's mouth and licking at it. This was not the frantic coming together they'd shared the last time. Gavin was building their passion slowly, rocking them together.

Davy sighed into Gavin's mouth with every rock of their hips. His stomach fluttered with a mix of butterflies and excitement. He'd never been touched so gently yet seduced so completely. Gavin could talk a mean game, but there was no way he was insincere in what they were doing. Gavin wasn't being rough and trying to get off, he was being considerate and taking care of Davy. *He's being* close *to you.* It was intimate. So intimate Davy wanted to cry because he'd not realized he'd never actually been touched by anyone in a way that made him feel cared for, not since the last hug he'd gotten from his mother. Davy could have done without the way Gavin was making his cock hum with pleasure and just drifted in the feeling of someone giving a shit. And he was stunned that of all people in the world making him feel this, it was Gavin Walker. It seemed like such a drastic switch in emotion from the last time he'd been in a heated moment with Gavin.

Gavin nipped Davy one more time before stilling himself and placing his forehead on Davy's to catch his breath. Davy was disappointed, chasing the kiss as Gavin pulled away. Damn if Gavin didn't look good, lips shining and swollen from their kissing. Gavin stood and held his hand out to Davy. Davy was done with objections. He'd been blue-balled last time, so his cock was more than onboard with everything that was going on. He knew he was reading too much into all this, so he needed to do as Gavin had done and just take what he was offering: a chance to get off. He figured he'd be pissed at himself when Gavin freaked out again, but if Davy could get off with another person for the first time in a very, very long time, then maybe all would not be wasted.

Davy took Gavin's hand and Gavin led the way to his bedroom. When Gavin flicked a light switch and flooded the small room with light, Davy was surprised again. There were black-and-white prints of stars from Hollywood past. Rock Hudson, Marilyn Monroe. A large subway poster of James Dean hung above the king-sized bed. There were model classic cars on most of the surfaces. Davy hadn't realized just how much Gavin's grandfather had influenced him, but it explained so much about his too-cool persona. Even when he was using his club-boy routine, he pulled off the *Rebel Without a Cause* attitude. Davy grinned at the thought of Gavin in a white T-shirt, cigarette pack wrapped in a sleeve with pomade slicking back his wild brown hair. Gavin was less an enigma with every moment Davy spent in his home, and Davy was beginning to hope he wasn't foolish in thinking that maybe, just maybe, Gavin was showing Davy his true self. Davy even let himself hope for a fraction of a second it wouldn't get snatched away.

Gavin pulled him into the room. Davy noticed he was blushing and a snort escaped, which got him a nasty scowl from Gavin. "What? You act like no one's been in your bed before." Now that almost *really* made Davy laugh.

"No."

"No, what?" Davy questioned. Gavin's face was challenging.

"No one has ever been in my room, much less my bed."

Davy was taken aback. "Oh. Sorry, I guess I just assumed." He felt bad for being flippant, but Gavin had to understand why he thought that. Gavin's shoulders slumped a little. Davy realized with surprise that he'd actually hurt Gavin.

"It's okay," Gavin said quietly. "I get why you'd think that. Guess the apple don't fall far from the tree." Gavin laughed at himself derisively.

Davy furrowed his brow, confused. Gavin pulled his hand away from Davy, squaring his shoulders, looking at Davy with an unreadable mask. Davy sighed sadly, wondering why *he* should feel bad, because he did. Gavin had been trying to fix things, had been so sweet, and was trying to prove himself—and by all accounts he had a little—and Davy had called him a whore. But Gavin had agreed. Davy didn't get what he'd meant when he said he'd not fallen far from the tree, though.

"Well, I guess this was too much. I'll take you home if you want," Gavin said as he straightened his beanie and started to walk out of the room. Davy felt like an ass, though he was sure he could think of reasons why Gavin deserved what he'd said. But for some reason, he didn't like the idea of hurting Gavin's feelings. *Maybe because I'm always the one that's hurt.*

Davy didn't know why that made any difference since it was Gavin himself who'd hurt him, but Davy just couldn't be cruel. And his body was rebelling with every step Gavin took away from him. The feeling was almost overwhelming.

Davy grabbed him by his bicep. "Don't go." Gavin turned and Davy saw a hurt-yet-hopeful gleam in his eyes before Gavin was able to hide it. Davy gave his best apologetic smile and stepped into Gavin's space. He wasn't sure what had come over him, but he wanted to give Gavin a reason not to run tomorrow. He wanted to prove himself too, and he knew maybe it made him naïve. Gavin's eyelids fluttered shut as Davy placed a sweet kiss on his closed lips. "I'm sorry. I didn't mean that. I'm so sorry, Gavin."

When Gavin's Adam's apple bobbed, his face scrunching to conceal some emotion, Davy felt emboldened. He'd make that emotion come out even if—Gavin gave a shuddering sigh as Davy placed his palm to his cheek. Yeah. That'd do it.

"Gavin, I don't think badly of you. It was a mean thing to assume. I was teasing, mostly, since you seemed embarrassed." Gavin was silent but Davy wanted to reassure him. "I don't think you're, like, a whore or anything, ya know?"

Gavin opened his eyes, looking incredulous. Davy snorted. "Okay, so I *know* you're no saint. I'm not an idiot, Gavin. But you're here. You showed me this side of you. I get it. You're a good guy."

Damn, that whiskey was good. Davy normally couldn't mollify his own inner voice much less another human being, but he was doing well right now. Or maybe it was because it was Gavin. Davy really wanted him to know that he might not get what made Gavin tick, but he did know he wasn't what he made himself look like in public.

Davy kissed Gavin again. For a moment Gavin's response was robotic, as though he was just going through the motions. That wouldn't do. Davy carded his fingers through Gavin's hair, knocking his hat to the floor. Gavin's shaggy brown hair was thicker than Davy imagined. He wrapped his arm around Gavin's back, pulled them together, and let Gavin slip his tongue into his mouth. Gavin melted into him with another shuddering sigh. Gavin wrapped his arms around Davy and held him tight as they kissed, and as they had the last time, started a steady rocking of their hips as their cocks hardened against each other. Davy grunted when Gavin started pushing him back toward the bed, and they fell back onto the mattress together, Gavin on top.

Gavin leaned up on his elbows, staring down into Davy's eyes. He placed a kiss on Davy's nose, his cheek. "I meant it. I've never had anyone in here. Ever. I'm not going to apologize for my past, but I hope you know I'm not using you like that. You're not just another hookup. I'd never have brought you here, never introduced you to Ray."

Davy heard the truth in those words and felt honored. He wasn't sure how the mood changed, but the air didn't only crackle with sex and chemistry, but a strong blanket of warmth and caring also seemed to be weaving around the two of them. Davy wasn't good at trusting his instincts where other people were concerned but there, in that moment, he decided Gavin was worth this risk. "I have an answer for you."

Gavin kissed Davy's lips again, then assessed him. "Answer to what?"

"You asked what I wanted, earlier. I know what I want." Davy tried to make his voice as certain as he could.

"Oh?"

"You, Gavin. No bullshit, though. I want us to figure out what this is between us, okay? If you think there *is* something between us." Davy knew he didn't sound sure.

Gavin ran his fingers down Davy's cheek. "There is definitely something here, Davy. I don't know why, but you make me want to be different. Hell, you make me want to be a good guy."

"I don't know who convinced you that you aren't good. But you are." Davy was certain of that. No one cared for their grandfather or was as loved as Gavin if they weren't good.

Gavin looked sad again, defeated. "Haven't you heard? I'm trouble."

Davy smiled and nipped Gavin's bottom lip. "Well, trouble might not be all bad." He bucked his hips up into Gavin, and Gavin rolled his eyes back in pleasure. "I think you should show me some of those 'other things' now."

"And I thought you were the shy little wallflower," Gavin teased.

Davy wrapped his arms around Gavin's waist and squeezed his firm ass. "Haven't you heard the old saying 'it's always the quiet ones'?"

"Indeed." Gavin smirked, then licked a path from Davy's throat to his ear, then nibbled on Davy's earlobe. Davy loved having his ears licked, gave an appreciative moan, and squirmed, his cock rearing against Gavin's. Gavin grunted and pushed his own cock against the friction.

Gavin sat up, tugging on Davy's shirt. "You. Naked. Now."

The fire burning in Gavin's gaze intimidated Davy. He didn't think he'd seen anything so intense in his life. It was a heady feeling, knowing he could get Gavin that worked up. Gavin reached down and ran a thumb over Davy's bottom lip. Davy shivered. No way he wasn't giving in to Gavin tonight.

So off went his clothes.

GAVIN STARED in awe after they both hurriedly stripped. Every inch of Davy was bared before him, and from his oversized feet to his flat belly to his embarrassed baby face, the boy was made for sex. Not just for sex but to be touched, loved, cherished. He was the perfect balance of hard and soft. Broad shoulders, arms and legs thick from heavy lifting and bike riding, but not like a gym bunny's. Soft honey-colored skin covered a slightly defined chest and the most beautifully protruding hipbones Gavin had ever seen.

And that cock. Gavin's mouth watered just at the thought of tasting Davy. He jumped Davy hungrily and started with sloppy kissing, licking into Davy's mouth aggressively. He pulled lightly at Davy's hair, exposing the column of Davy's neck. Gavin licked his way down, nibbling when he reached the collarbone. Davy was squirming, cock jumping with every kiss to his heated skin. Gavin briefly stopped to kiss each rosy nipple, then continued his descent. Davy wasn't making much more noise than the occasional whimper that came out with a heavy breath.

Gavin wanted this to be special. He wanted to show Davy this could be right. He didn't know what had made Davy so important, why he'd introduced Davy to Ray or invited him to his room. But he wanted Davy's approval. He wanted someone to think he had goodness in him. To prove he wasn't his mother's fucking child.

When Davy had said the words, said he thought Gavin was good, Gavin's heart had burst with joy. He'd almost wept. And Gavin Walker did *not* weep. Or swoon. But that was exactly what he'd done when Davy had kissed him. And here he was, *making love* to Davy. The whole situation was unnerving, but he wouldn't back down. Something inside him said Davy was worth it. He wanted to get this right.

So Gavin took his time. He laved Davy's navel. Davy reached down and ran his fingers through Gavin's hair, moaning. Gavin smiled to himself, happy he'd pleased Davy. He moved to those sexy hipbones and gently bit each one, then licked and kissed them to soothe the bites. He got carried away and noticed a love mark had arisen on one, then looked up to apologize, but Davy was looking down at him through half-lidded eyes, mouth open and breathing heavy.

"Sorry about the hickeys." *Not really.* He liked the idea of marking Davy. Davy's response was to grab Gavin and pull him up into a steamy, bone-melting kiss. Gavin couldn't remember a tastier kiss or feeling more perfect lying naked with someone. It was a revelation. His chest tightened at the rightness of every moment of them lying in each other's arms, grinding their cocks together, kissing and touching.

Gavin reached his hand between them and wrapped their cocks together in his fist. "Thrust, Davy."

And Davy did. Gavin didn't even hold back the moan that came from somewhere deep inside his chest. Davy placed a hand on Gavin's face. Gavin kissed his palm, then sucked Davy's thumb into his mouth as he thrust into his own fist. They set up an awkward but delicious rhythm together. The feeling of their legs touching and cocks thrusting in the tight confines of Gavin's fist was making Gavin's cock ache. His brain registered their balls rubbing together, and the intimacy was something for which Gavin was unprepared.

Eyes closed, head back, Davy's face was beautiful as he got closer and closer to his release. Gavin wanted to remember that blissful abandon forever. He knew he'd never know another Davy Cooper in all his days.

Davy's eyes flew open, jaw dropped. Quietly he started chanting, "Oh, oh, oh. Gavin. Oh."

Gavin's balls drew up at the sound of his name on Davy's lips. "Fuck."

They thrust faster together. Davy reached around, gripped Gavin's ass, and pulled him into the thrusting harder as though he was trying to fuse their bodies together. With his other hand on the nape of Gavin's neck, Davy pulled Gavin in for a kiss that was full of puffy breaths and saliva and battling tongues. Then, in a mix between a grunt and a moan, Davy rolled his body inward, sweetly tucking his face into Gavin's chest as he spilled. Gavin continued thrusting and pulling their cocks, and Davy gasped with each shot of white seed between their bellies.

The feel of Davy tucked safely to his chest and the smell of them together made Gavin's balls pull up tight against Davy's, the slide of their most intimate body parts finishing him off. Gavin held Davy tight to him as his seed joined Davy's between their bodies.

They lay together, Gavin on top, legs entangled, sticky and sweaty for a moment. The room was silent save for the sound of their heavy breathing. Davy surprised Gavin by kissing him lightly on the neck and giving Gavin a gentle squeeze with the arm he still had around his waist. Gavin pushed up to look down at him. Davy looked so serene, without a worry in the world. Gavin knew he was a goner. He'd never wanted to stay close in the same bed with someone he'd hooked up with, ever. He'd never been so fulfilled by just rubbing off with someone, much less lying in their arms. But this time he felt as if he could fly, as though he'd actually found true release with Davy. It was strange, but he thought he might like getting used to the feeling.

He leaned down and kissed Davy between his eyebrows. "You, sir, are sexy."

Davy scoffed and blushed. Gavin loved knowing the blush went all the way to Davy's chest, even with his skin being a darker honey color. Gavin would see that in his mind's eye every time Davy blushed now.

"You are, Davy. That—*that* was...."

"Awesome?" Davy asked.

His tone was hopeful, which made Gavin laugh. And wasn't that the damnedest feeling? Kissing and holding each other and laughing and talking. Was this what sex was really supposed to be like?

No. This is what making love is. He quieted at that thought. "Yes, Davy. It was awesome." And he meant it.

He got out of bed, mind racing, and went to the bathroom for a towel. When he came back, he moved to wipe Davy's stomach off. His dick perked up a bit seeing their come commingling on Davy's flat belly, then threatened to get hard again immediately as he wiped down Davy's thick cock.

Gavin's brain wasn't quite catching up with his horny body, though. He was nervous about all the feelings he had for Davy. He feared hurting him, and that was something he didn't know how to handle. Neither Gavin nor his bed partners ever stuck around for cleanup, much less cuddling, so he didn't know how the hell to handle himself right then.

Until he saw that Davy had lost his serene expression and was now chewing his bottom lip, seemingly uncertain. *Shit.* Gavin did the only thing he knew to do then, the only thing he wanted to do.

He crawled into bed and pulled Davy into his arms. He settled the covers over them, and after a kiss to Davy's temple, which was warm and soft and smelled of Davy, he drifted into a peaceful sleep.

CHAPTER TWELVE

DAVY WOKE slowly to the sensation of fingers fluttering over his chest, down his belly. His body shivered at the light contact. When he could focus clearly, he saw an obvious question in Gavin's mischievous eyes. Gavin leaned in, placing a gentle kiss on Davy's lips. His hips canted, searching out the hand that never came quite close enough to his hardness.

"Gavin, please." He knew his voice was whining, but damn, Gavin's restraint was appreciated but unnecessary.

Gavin's warm body pulled away after he gave a naughty chuckle. Then suddenly his cock was warm and wet and throbbing. A delicious friction pulled a tingling from deep inside his belly. His balls felt as though they were being sucked through his cock. His eyes popped open when a hum from Gavin sent nerve-shocking vibrations through his entire body.

He almost came instantly when he saw the wicked gleam in Gavin's eyes and Gavin's sexy lips wrapped around his cock. Nope. This was definitely not a dream. Gavin was artfully taking care of Davy's morning wood, and Davy could do nothing but moan in satisfaction as Gavin used a hand to roll Davy's balls in their sac.

Gavin's head bobbed up and down. Davy had never seen anything as arousing as the column of his flesh disappearing into Gavin's mouth. Gavin looked as though he was attempting a smile before he swallowed and took Davy deep into his throat. It took only a gentle massage of

Gavin's throat muscles and another tug to Davy's balls to make Davy pant, "Gonna come! Fuck. Gavin."

Gavin didn't come up, though. He stroked Davy's cock again with his throat and rolled Davy's balls as Davy erupted. Davy groaned as spurt after spurt of his seed shot deep into Gavin's throat. Davy's gaze never left where Gavin's lips were pressed around his cock, which was buried to the hilt inside his lover.

Gavin licked and suckled the head of Davy's cock, cleaning him, until Davy could handle it no more. When Gavin came up for a kiss, Davy was breathless and sated, and Gavin could probably have gotten anything he wanted in that moment.

Davy loved tasting himself in Gavin's mouth. He couldn't imagine anything more erotic or more perfect than Gavin on top of him, knowing he was carrying a private piece of Davy inside him for only them to know about.

"I'll do you," Davy said once he'd gotten his breathing back to normal.

Gavin kissed him again. "No need. I got off just blowing you. I've wanted to taste you for so long. It was so not a disappointment."

Davy knew he blushed. He wasn't sure which made him hornier, but his cock attempted to rise again. Gavin clasped it in his hand and chuckled again. "I like how you respond to me, Davy."

Davy was not good at dirty talk, so he just thrust into Gavin's hand, but before he started anything else, he happened to catch a glimpse of the clock on the bedside table. He let out an unhappy whimper. "Damn."

Gavin stopped what he was doing. "What's wrong?"

"My uncle is coming into town today. He comes once a month to check up on me. He'll be at my apartment in just a couple of hours and it's a wreck. I need to go back and clean up. Soon."

"Well, I guess we'll just have to pick this up later." Gavin dropped a chaste peck against Davy's lips, then rolled off the bed to grab the towel he'd discarded the night before. He wiped his cock and Davy's leg where Gavin had rubbed himself off while blowing him. Davy so badly wanted to pick up where they'd left off immediately after seeing that.

He was still amazed how much Gavin turned him on and vice versa. Davy couldn't imagine why Gavin was so attracted to the awkward and shy kid from the soda shop, but he knew they were fucking hot together. He'd never felt anything like what they'd done the night before, and was even more surprised when Gavin seemed to stop whatever freak-out he'd been having after they'd finished and pulled Davy close. Davy had almost left during the night, not wanting to see Gavin flip out in the morning, but that was obviously not going to happen. *Yet.*

"Want coffee? I can make some breakfast."

Davy tried to tell Gavin not to trouble himself, but after he'd finished showering, Gavin corralled Davy into the kitchen where Ray was sitting at a table in the breakfast nook reading a newspaper. Ray looked about as stunned to see Davy stumble into the kitchen as Davy felt at still being there for breakfast. Gavin made Davy sit at the table, where Ray stared at Davy, making him squirm. When Gavin set a cup of coffee in front of Davy, then started scrambling eggs, whistling at the stove, Ray harrumphed and disappeared behind his paper again with a knowing grin.

Before Davy had time to put much thought into what Ray did and didn't know about his night—and morning—with Gavin, Gavin placed plates of eggs, sausage, and toast in front of them. Davy and Ray eyed each other again, Ray smirking, looking so much like Gavin. Well, Davy supposed it was the other way around, technically, and Gavin looked so much like Ray that no one could deny their being related. Gavin pulled out a chair next to Davy and sat down with his own plate, then leaned to kiss Davy on the temple. Ray broke out into a bright smile, looking between them. When Davy blushed and chewed his lip, Gavin rolled his eyes, chuckling, and Ray laughed out loud. The laugh made Davy feel light. The world seemed right while Davy sat at that table with these two men.

"Oh, yeah, I like this one, boy. You did real good," Ray said before tucking in to his food.

Davy looked to Gavin, trying to gauge his response. Gavin took a bite of his toast and winking, smirked at Davy. Damn these men for smirking their way into his heart. It scared the shit out of him while still making everything seem as it should.

"Best part of being finished with that damn radiation is being able to taste this food you whip up," Ray said to Gavin.

The room silenced as if something had hit a Mute button on the world. Gavin's shoulders squared and Davy could feel the despair radiating off him. While Davy did agree that this was an amazing breakfast—*who makes eggs taste like a miracle?*—he was stunned by the mention of Ray's cancer. Ray realized his faux pas immediately and reached out his hand to Gavin. Gavin jumped up from the table and dumped his breakfast in the trash, then disappeared down the stairs to his room without a word. Ray turned to Davy, face scrunched up apologetically.

Davy wasn't sure why he found it so easy to comfort these Walker men, but he patted Ray's hand that was still on the table. "It's okay. He's just sad. He's going to miss you."

Ray shook his head mournfully. "I know. That boy hasn't had it easy. I tried to fight it for him. He needs watching." Ray pinned Davy with a pleading stare. "I've never seen him bring home anyone, much less introduce him, have him sleep over, and cook for him. I can't say as I've ever heard that boy whistle like fucking Snow White while he worked in the kitchen. I know it's a lot to ask, especially knowing my Gavin, but I'm hoping you'll consider being around for him, because I won't be soon."

Davy's chest ached at the thought of losing this man, and he'd only just met Ray. He couldn't imagine how Gavin felt. All he could do was nod in agreement. He could always *try* for Gavin's sake.

Ray seemed fine with Davy's response. "You're a good kid, Davy."

He wasn't sure how Ray could make that assessment, but he didn't contradict the man.

Gavin came up the stairs shortly thereafter, showered and in jeans, a T-shirt, and his ubiquitous beanie. Davy couldn't help the fluttering that burst to life in his stomach, but it was pleasant and he didn't mind.

"Ready to head out, Davy?"

Gavin still didn't seem too chipper, but he was obviously in a better state of mind than he was before.

"Yeah. What should I do with my dish?" Davy held up his empty plate. "It was great, by the way. Thanks for breakfast."

Gavin beamed at him. And there went Davy's breath right out his lungs again. *You may just kill me this way, Gavin.*

"I'll get these dishes. You boys just go have some fun," Ray said, taking Davy's plate and heading for the sink.

"You need anything while I'm out?" Gavin asked.

Ray just waved him off and Gavin motioned for Davy to follow him.

"It was nice to meet you, sir," Davy said before he went after Gavin.

Ray turned to him and nodded. "It's Ray, boy. And don't be a stranger."

Davy patted his shoulder fondly. "Wouldn't dream of it."

DAVY WAS amused at Gavin's offense when he told Gavin he didn't have to stay and help clean his apartment. Gavin had only grunted his disapproval, then bustled into the kitchen to do dishes. Davy was oddly pleased every time he looked up to see Gavin still there doing domestic tasks. It felt so very couple-ish. They worked well together and the work got finished quickly. Davy hated Gavin seeing the mess he accumulated through the week and felt guilty whenever Gavin grumbled about how untidy something was, but any time he'd told Gavin to stop what he was doing he got a glare, so he'd resisted even trying anymore.

When they'd finished, Gavin ran out for takeout. They'd finished in time to enjoy a lunch together with a while to spare. Uncle Drew had text-messaged to say he was still an hour away by the time they'd finished eating, so they sat back on the couch, shoulder to shoulder, looking around, pleased at the immaculately clean apartment.

"Thanks for helping," Davy offered.

"Shut up. It wasn't a big deal." Davy held back a smile.

"You didn't have to," Davy persisted.

"Whatever. I got to hang out with you." Gavin stared at a spot on the wall.

Davy let his smile break free. That was exactly the reason he suspected Gavin had stayed, but it was nice to hear the words.

"Well, I really appreciate it," Davy said. He leaned over and kissed the corner of Gavin's mouth.

Gavin looked at him sideways. "You're pretty good at that."

Davy furrowed his brow. "At what?"

"Making me tell you what I'm feeling."

Davy scoffed. "Nobody can make you do anything."

Gavin shot him a highly unamused glare.

Davy laughed. "Maybe you just *want* to tell me those things, eh?"

Gavin started to protest, Davy could tell, but he stopped himself and shook his head. "Yeah. I guess. God help me, I want you to know how much I enjoy being around you."

Davy took Gavin's hand and quietly said, "I liked spending time with you too."

Davy rolled his eyes at the sudden smugness that took over Gavin's face. Davy put a stop to that by punching him in the arm.

"Hey!" Gavin rubbed his arm where Davy had hit him. "What was that for?"

"Every time I think you're an ass that's going to happen."

"I better buy shoulder pads," Gavin deadpanned.

"Probably." Davy stood and started picking up the empty carryout containers from their lunch. When he returned, Gavin was chewing the inside of his cheek as though he had a question he didn't know how to ask. "What's up?"

Gavin was quiet for another moment before asking, "So what's the deal with your uncle checking on you so often?"

Davy sighed, then plopped down on the daybed next to Gavin. "He worries about me. He lives in Ellensburg, thankfully. If he lived here he'd be here every damn day."

"But why?"

"Oh, it's nothing major. Ever since my mom died, he feels guilty that he couldn't be around for me. He thinks I'm completely incapable of functioning. He's not the only one, unfortunately."

Gavin was thoughtfully silent. Davy thought maybe he was finished with his questions, but Davy didn't know what to say next.

"Is there a reason? Are you sick?"

Oh, Gavin.

Davy placed a hand on Gavin's thigh and rubbed it, trying to silence whatever monster was playing in Gavin's head. "No, babe. I'm fine." Gavin's eyes widened in surprise at the endearment. Davy blushed and shoved on because he wasn't sure why he'd called Gavin that. "My mom was agoraphobic. Severely. She'd always been anxious, but after my dad was killed in a robbery, she went off the deep end. I was so young I don't really remember much before that, but I do remember her getting much more strict. She wouldn't let me go out to play at first. Then she stopped letting me leave for groceries. She started homeschooling me, but I couldn't go to any of the homeschool group meetings. My socializing went out the window before I was ten. Hence my inability to be a normal member of society."

Gavin scowled at him. "Shut up. You're fine."

Davy wanted to kiss Gavin for sticking up for him. He had been picked on quite a bit for his shyness. It warmed him to his toes to hear someone other than his mother or Uncle Drew tell him he wasn't a total freak. And to hear it from Gavin was enough to give him wings.

"Well, she tried to stop it, but I finally got Uncle Drew to talk her into letting me get a job at Bart's when I was sixteen. He said I needed to learn practical skills."

"You've been there six years?"

"Yeah."

"And you're not a manager?" Gavin sounded offended on Davy's behalf.

"Gavin, I *am* a manager. *The* manager. Haven't you noticed how often I'm there?" Gavin looked completely surprised. "I have been for a year." Davy laughed when he realized "You actually hit on me the first time on my second day as manager. I'm the general manager. There's an assistant under me who works nights, but it's mostly me and the owner, Henry, running things. It pays well enough until I finish school."

"You don't mind that your mom kept you in a bubble for so long?"

It was certainly not the first time Davy had heard that question. But definitely the first time he'd wanted to answer it honestly.

"I struggled a lot to forgive her after she died, and I had a hard time adjusting. That's why my uncle checks on me. Those first few months were ugly. I didn't know shit about paying bills or apartment hunting or what areas of town to move to. All I knew was even with my inheritance and my job I couldn't afford to keep her apartment."

"Wow. But you forgave her?" Gavin seemed perplexed by the idea.

"Of course. She was my mom. Eventually I realized that, though it wasn't fair, she did it all out of love. Some parents do worse things out of love. Am I still bitter? At times, yes, but she did her best with the situation she was handed."

Gavin hummed his response and sat silently. Davy hated to ask, but he was curious now. "Are you having trouble forgiving your mom for something?"

Davy thought for a moment Gavin wouldn't answer, but finally he spoke. "It's different."

"Okay." Davy was a bit annoyed that he couldn't get a straight answer since he'd been so honest, but maybe the damage was deeper than just an overbearing mother.

"I never knew my dad." It was a matter-of-fact statement. Gavin sounded as though he had no opinion on that one way or the other.

"I'm sorry?" Davy didn't know what to say to that.

"Nah. No big. I had Ray. He was awesome, even though Carmen did her best to keep him away."

"Carmen?"

"My mom. If you can call her that."

Davy didn't say anything. He just let Gavin figure out in his own time what he wanted to tell. Quite frankly, Davy was still on overload from the last two days, so he thought he might fall over from shock if Gavin actually shared his past.

"My mom's a drunk," Gavin said angrily.

Okay. Now he might fall over from shock.

Gavin nodded as though he had made up his mind about something. "She spent my whole life talking about how she never wanted to be a mother. She had new men over all the time. She bitched about how much her parents expected of her. Then when I got a job to save up for college, I got my first bank account and she'd take money from it to pay for her booze. When my grandma died and we both got trusts, she blew through hers in less than a year and tried to get at mine, but Ray made sure he was the secondary on that account so she couldn't touch it. She was so mad. She made me buy my own school clothes and everything from that point on. I just kept working and putting away to move here when it came time for university."

"I'm so sorry" was all Davy could think to say when Gavin stopped talking.

"I was an idiot. I still loved her. I mean, she's my mom."

"Of course." Davy rubbed his knuckles down Gavin's cheek.

Gavin flinched, then jumped up from the couch and started pacing. "No. I was stupid. And I want you to know this because I want you to know why I have been such an idiot with you, so just let me tell you this because I don't think I'll have the nerve again."

"Okay," Davy said encouragingly. Davy could feel the pain vibrating off Gavin, echoing through the sparse studio, bruising his own heart.

"It may seem weird, but Carmen was always jealous of me. She *made* me call her Carmen. She tried to fit in with my friends. She hit on the guys, which was humiliating. She hated that Ray and I were so close. She'd bitch for days about how I had it so much easier than her; how everyone loved me and that even her own dad liked me more than her." Gavin stopped pacing and stared at the ground, running his fingers through his hair while he gathered his composure. "She was so pissed when I came out. Not because I was gay, but because my friends were accepting, Ray was accepting. She was furious, but she didn't show it to anyone. She acted like the cool, accepting mom."

Gavin sat back down on the couch but didn't look at Davy. He hugged himself, and Davy ached with the need to touch him but thought better of it.

"She really didn't have a problem with me being gay—she just had a problem with me. So I stayed. I hoped she'd change, and I guess I had developed a guilt complex. She'd blamed me for her drinking for so long that I felt like all those DUIs were my fault, all the broken relationships. She even made me feel guilty for having a boyfriend that didn't leave me."

"You don't have to say any more." Davy was dying for Gavin. Gavin's pain was like an entity taking on its own life the more he talked.

"No. I want you to know."

Davy didn't know why Gavin was sharing so much, but he let him finish.

"I figured even with my savings and trust fund it'd be best to at least finish up at the local community college, plus I could still be with Max for two more years before we headed off to a university. I could save money and be with my 'high school sweetheart.'" Gavin put air quotes around the latter and snarled the words. "Well, Max was a huge closet case. His dad was a total dick, but we were together for three years. Until the summer after our freshman year of college. His dad had started figuring out we weren't just friends, and Max started getting the idea maybe he should get a girlfriend. He always said it'd be easier if there were just a girl that looked like me. I always took that as a weird compliment, a safety net for our relationship."

Davy didn't know how because it shouldn't have been his first guess, but to his horror, he guessed the next part of Gavin's story and was nauseous before the words came out of Gavin's mouth.

Gavin sucked in a breath as if he were diving into the deep end and forged on. "I came home to find my mother and Max fucking on the couch."

Davy felt as though the wind had been punched out of him. And it hadn't even happened to him. Who did something that sick?

"I'll give it to Max. At least he had the decency to look as guilty as he should have. He tried to apologize for months. Honestly, I loved him, but who can forgive their boyfriend cheating with their mom, ya know? And Carmen? She said I'd had it too easy and it was about time I learned I couldn't get everything. I packed my shit that night while she was out getting drunk and caught a really expensive flight out of the local airport and came straight to Ray's. I even left my car behind. I didn't care. I just wanted to get the hell out of there forever."

Davy stared at Gavin. He had no clue what to say to Gavin's admission, but he understood being gun-shy after that. He probably had never spoken to another person about this, and here Gavin was trying to be someone Davy could be with.

"Oh my God, Gavin. I'm so sorry."

Davy thought *Fuck it* and pulled Gavin to him. Gavin was so obviously wrung out that he didn't even fight against Davy's embrace. They sat silently for a long while; Davy pretending he didn't know Gavin's trembling and the wetness on his shoulders were evidence of Gavin silently crying. Davy had never felt as though he wanted to rip someone apart limb from limb, much less a woman. But if he saw Carmen Walker right then, he might do just that.

When Gavin had quieted, Davy kissed the top of his head and said, "I'm so sorry, Gavin. You didn't deserve that. I just hope you know I'll be here, okay? I am here. I know I made that dig last night, but I meant it when I said I want us to be together and I'm so happy to know you for as long as I get to know you."

Gavin looked up at him with red-rimmed eyes, and Davy almost cried himself when Gavin sniffled pitifully. "I'm sorry I dumped all that. I've never told anyone that. I didn't even tell Ray about Max."

"Probably best. He'd have killed her, I'm sure. You mean the world to him, Gavin."

Gavin smiled. "Yeah. He's the greatest."

"You're pretty great too." Davy kissed Gavin's last remaining tears away. Davy felt privileged to see him like this. He hated it, but he was so glad to be the person Gavin finally released his burden on.

"Did I scare you off?" Gavin asked.

"You mean the part where you proved how strong you were or the part where you trusted me with something that hurt you so much?"

Gavin shook his head sadly. "The part where I showed that I'm not a badass. I'm just like her. I—"

"Stop right there, Gav. You are nothing like her. You're kind and you treat your friends well and you never stopped making up to me any wrong you felt you'd done to me. I could fall for you, and it's scary because everything scares me a little. But maybe we can be scared and strong together?" Davy was convinced he could do just that if Gavin was onboard to give it a try.

Gavin smiled a watery smile that made Davy tremble.

"I'm falling for you too, Soda Shop Boy."

Davy rolled his eyes at the nickname and kissed Gavin on the lips. He didn't know how he had done it, but he'd brought a smile back to Gavin's face. He liked being strong for Gavin, though. He hoped he could live up to Ray's request to be around for Gavin when Ray was gone.

Davy was beginning to think he might always want to be around for Gavin Walker. And that thought wasn't very scary at all.

CHAPTER
THIRTEEN

DAVY SEEMED shocked but pleased when Gavin stuck around to at least be introduced to Davy's uncle Drew. Drew had to have known something was off with Gavin's mood, but he'd been polite and kind. Gavin was surprised how close the man was to their age. The man had been as surprised as Gavin when Davy introduced Gavin as his boyfriend, but like Gavin, Drew had seemed happy to hear Davy was dating someone.

Gavin had no clue why he'd dumped all his garbage on Davy. He felt guilty and vulnerable to the point of being raw, but he also felt light. Ray had shared some of his burden, as had Gavin's friends. They had all been so great, but Davy—Davy was this unexpected safe place. It had been so easy to share his most humiliating, heartsick moment.

Gavin was coming to find that even in his shyness and awkwardness, Davy was a force of nature with a surprising, quiet strength. As much as he didn't want to trust how he was feeling, he'd seen the moment when Davy had opened his heart to Gavin, and Gavin had felt his heart tether to Davy's.

It was fucking scary. But it felt right. Gavin needed a moment to get his thoughts about it together, so he'd bowed out after introductions and drove around the city aimlessly for hours before returning home. He'd steeled his resolve to dive headfirst into what had developed between himself and Davy. And if there was one thing anyone could tell you about Gavin Walker, it was that when he made up his mind, he was stubborn and fought to stay on that path. And the path to Davy had way too much hope on it to make him want to wander off. Gavin was out of his depth. He had gone years without getting emotionally involved with someone in the way he was with Davy, but he had Davy now, and he didn't want either of them to be alone anymore. More than anything, Gavin didn't want to hurt anymore, and he didn't want anyone else to use or hurt the pureness that existed in Davy.

Gavin knew getting to this point had taken a push or two, but he'd meant it when he told Davy he cared about him. Gavin knew that for certain when Davy said he cared too. Gavin had almost flown apart from the joy of the confession. He was filled with hope. Hope... and love.

Gavin sat for a long while in his truck, staring at his grandfather's house, unable to move at the realization of how much he really had fallen in love with Davy. Not that Gavin was quite ready to say those three words, but the truth was undeniable. They hadn't just had sex. They'd made love. And it had made Gavin feel more wanted, more special than he knew how to comprehend.

Gavin was finished fighting. He hoped Davy was finished too. But he could wait it out, either way. After all, look how long he'd waited just to get Davy to have a coffee with him, even when Gavin didn't do "coffee" and all it implied, unless coffee was a metaphor for a blowjob in the bathroom.

Gavin shook his head as he scolded himself for being such an idiot. And he felt okay admitting he'd acted like an idiot and done exactly what he'd not wanted. He'd let his mother continue to affect his life from a million miles away. And wasn't it shocking how quickly he became that self-aware?

A knock on his window startled Gavin from his thoughts. Devon stood outside the truck looking amused. Gavin flipped him off and opened the door.

"Fucker," Gavin said with no heat to the word.

"Sorry, Gav."

"What's up, Devon?"

"I wanted to know how it went with Davy. I was about to bust not talking to the guys about what a dick you had been."

Gavin scowled at Devon and punched him in the arm, getting a "Hey!"

"Come on in and see Ray, so long as you're here."

Gavin led the way into the house. Devon had made his way in to see Ray before Gavin had shut the door and taken off his shoes. When Gavin walked into the sitting room, Devon and Ray both went silent and stared at him expectantly.

"What?" Gavin shrunk under their gazes.

"Well…," Devon said, rotating his hand in front of him, gesturing for Gavin to speak up.

"Well what?" Gavin feigned ignorance, which got him two disbelieving harrumphs that were eerily similar. Gavin was beginning to think he'd let his friends spend too much time around the old guy. He glared at them both.

"Spill it, Gav. Did you make up with Pretty Boy?" Devon pushed.

"And how," Ray stated jovially, eyes crinkling in the corners with smile lines.

Gavin gestured to Ray. "The gossip queen there will give you a play-by-play if you bribe him with a foot rub. I'm going to change."

Gullible Devon eyed Ray's proffered feet warily. Gavin started to leave when Ray said, "I'll even tell you about how that Davy boy stayed the whole night and how crazy in love our boy is."

Gavin halted in his tracks and turned his surprised gaze on Ray. Ray held a hand up to stop the protest Gavin never intended to give. "Don't deny it, boy. I suspected that the first time you talked about him. I knew it was different, but then I saw you with that boy. You were different. All's I can say is, it's about damn time you finally found someone to knock your socks off. And that Davy has got you tripping over yourself in love."

Devon started laughing, but it died in his throat when Gavin smiled shyly and said, "Yeah. Yeah, I think I love him."

That seemed to take Ray and Devon by surprise. Ray sat up straight in his chair, and Gavin realized he had struck the man dumb for the first time ever. Ray and Devon both looked at each other, then back to Gavin.

Devon, like a puppy wagging with happiness, bounded over to Gavin and hugged him, lifting him a few inches off the ground and squeezing the breath out of him.

"Dude, really? Ohmigod! This is so great! I knew it!" Devon set him back down.

Gavin straightened his shirt, flustered, as Devon continued pounding him on the back. When Gavin noticed Ray, he was practically glowing. That seeped deep into Gavin's soul. He knew Ray had been worried about him a lot lately, but he didn't realize just how much until he saw how Ray was reacting to him finally getting his head out of his own ass. Ray gave him a pleased nod.

"And Davy? What does he say?"

Gavin realized he'd almost forgotten Devon was still there until he spoke again, even though the guy's hand was still on his shoulder. "Oh, uh, I haven't told him yet."

"What?" Devon punched Gavin in the arm.

"Shit, dude!" Gavin rubbed his shoulder and flicked Devon's nose.

"You two are idiots," Ray grumbled.

"I just figured out that's what it was, okay?" Gavin defended.

Devon looked properly apologetic. "Oh, I guess that's why you looked all dreamy sitting out there in your truck."

"I was so not 'dreamy.'"

Ray harrumphed *again* and Devon objected with a "Whatever."

"You were mooning over the boy all night. Janie couldn't stop going on about how cute you boys were."

"How enlightened," Gavin said drily.

"Stop being a di— Well, stop being yourself," Devon said. "We are just all really happy for you. You've been so down since you moved here."

"Everybody needs love," Ray said as though the subject was closed. "So, Devon, how's school?"

"Well, it's okay. Gavin's been a big help in Macro...."

Gavin sat, listening to them catch up. He felt all warm and tingly, and a huge part of him wanted to wait for the other shoe to drop before doing anything drastic like admitting anything other than what he already had to Davy. But Gavin felt surprisingly calm for what he'd just admitted out loud for the first time. So today he'd admitted it to two of the most important people in his life, as well as himself. He supposed even with the good stuff, admitting it was the first step.

GAVIN TAPPED his pen against his desk in class, eventually calling enough attention to his impatience that his Art History professor paused her lecture and peered through her half-moon glasses at him. "Somewhere more pressing you should be, Mr. Walker?"

Of course he'd call attention to himself in his one class that was small enough that the professor knew him by name. He gave his most charming smile and apologized, which she didn't buy at all, but she continued on. He checked his phone every two minutes. He was ready to get out of the lecture hall. He was meeting the boys and Davy for dinner, and it was going to be the first time they'd all hung out since he and Davy had patched things up a little over a month earlier. Sure, they'd all seen each other in groups of three or four at a time, but no more than that because Gavin was obviously not hitting the clubs with the guys anymore, which shocked the hell out of them. But, at this point everyone knew the score between Gavin and Davy.

He was eager to see how everyone handled the situation. He'd not had anything resembling a relationship since he'd moved to Seattle three years earlier. Everyone seemed okay with the idea of him and Davy being a couple, and why shouldn't they? But Gavin was still nervous. And Gavin was never nervous. This was all new to him, completely beyond his ken.

He still hadn't even admitted to anyone other than Ray and Devon that he was in love with Davy. And at this point, he could say he was in love with complete certainty. In the last two weeks, they'd spent nights together both at Davy's apartment and Gavin's house. Davy had come to a few more boys' nights and had even driven Janie to church in Ray's old Cadillac the previous Sunday when neither her grandson nor Gavin were available.

Gavin was still in awe of Davy and how easily and quietly the man fit right into his life, his arms, and his heart. But how wouldn't he? The guy was all patience and calming steadfastness. Davy had stopped being awkward around Gavin long ago, speaking openly and animatedly about his interest in Gavin's studies and family. It was as though something had totally changed, and Gavin was still a little afraid to admit that the very hidden romantic in him wondered if Davy might not be *The One*. He knew that was an antiquated ideal and that guys his age didn't usually think that way, but what could he say? He was raised old-school.

But to think Davy was *The One* seemed a bit much, especially with having only officially known each other a few months. But Ray didn't seem to think so when Gavin had admitted it during one of their whiskey heart-to-hearts where Ray had also shared that his prognosis was worse than they thought, with only months left and the clock ticking fast. Ray had said, with eyes a bit too bright for Gavin's comfort, that he was happy for Gavin and that of course he'd want to find *The One*, not because he was old-school, but because he had an old soul. And for all of Davy's innocence and naïveté, Gavin thought much the same of him.

Then he wondered when the hell he'd become such a sap.

Finally, the professor called an end to the class. Gavin was the first person to bolt from the building and rushed to his truck. When he got to the restaurant they'd agreed on for dinner, he was the last to arrive. Of course. He made his way to the very large corner booth they'd managed to snag in the back of the restaurant. Everyone at the table had a large margarita in front of them and enough chips and *queso* for three families.

"Gavin!" Mason was the first to notice him as Gavin approached the table.

Davy looked up with such open adoration Gavin's whole world zoomed in on him. Gavin slid into the seat beside Davy and placed a peck on his cheek. The whole table erupted in "Awwww." Gavin didn't give a shit. Davy blushed furiously, but he never lost his smile.

Fucking beautiful.

Gavin directed his attention to his friends. "What's up, guys?"

100

Sean had his arm around Mason's shoulders, but somehow that didn't surprise him. Davy and Gavin had discussed the possibility of them getting together. It was pretty damn obvious they were getting closer and closer lately. Devon was beaming at Gavin, his pretty face the shade of red that was the telltale sign that he was well on his way to intoxication.

Then there was Nate. His face was set in a sneer, and he looked away as soon as Gavin made eye contact. Gavin felt kind of bad. He considered Nate a friend, but the guy knew the score between them. There was no reason to be a dick.

Gavin couldn't have been more pleased with how the dinner went. His nerves had been for naught. They'd all joked and had an awesome time. They'd embarrassed Davy after a few margaritas, trying to get info about his and Gavin's sex life. Then the tables got turned on Mason and Sean, who suddenly got very coy. Gavin knew that when Devon had gotten reduced to his random drunk giggles when no one had said anything funny that the night was drawing to an end.

The only one who didn't seemed to be enjoying himself was Nate. He was a bitchy guy, but not usually this bitchy. Nate had ignored a few direct questions from Davy and made digs about PDAs when Davy had put his hand on Gavin's knee under the table. Gavin got annoyed, but Davy had squeezed his knee and shook his head whenever Gavin had begun to say anything. That hand on his knee made Gavin's whole body calm, as if Davy's touch were a mood stabilizer. Gavin *would* deal with Nate later, regardless of what Davy thought on the matter. Everyone had given Nate the stink eye at some point for some of his rude comments because it was just weird to see anyone be rude to Davy.

"Dude, lay off," Gavin snapped at Nate. Nate just acted like he had no idea what he was talking about. "Whatever. Time for the check?" When everyone agreed the time had come to part ways, Sean signaled the waitress for the check.

Gavin excused himself to go to the restroom. When he arrived back at the table, Davy and Mason were missing, Devon looked stupefied, and Sean was doing his best impression of his Latino mother, laying into Nate, who looked entirely unaffected and unimpressed. They weren't fighting loud enough to draw attention to themselves, but Gavin knew them well enough to know shit was going down.

101

"What the fuck is going on?" Gavin asked.

Sean turned on Gavin, pointing at Nate with a growl. "This asshole was a total dick to Davy and it made Davy completely lose his shit."

"*What?*" Gavin snarled at Nate.

"I was just telling the truth."

"Whatever! You're a total douche-bag motherfucker!" Sean yelled.

A waitress came over with the check and wisely didn't bother to get involved when she seemed to notice the tension at the table.

"What happened?" Gavin snapped.

"Nate here talked trash to Davy. Total trash. Davy didn't want us to notice that it hurt his feelings, so he said he'd wait for you at the car and cut out."

Gavin got in Nate's face. The only sign Nate was intimidated was the smallest flinch when Gavin put his finger in his face and said with deadly calm, "You. I will deal with you later." He turned to Sean. "Davy's still here?"

Sean nodded, still looking at Nate in disgust. "Yes. He's waiting for you at your truck. Mason went to talk to him." He handed Gavin a wad of cash.

"What's this?" Gavin asked.

"Davy being Davy left this ridiculous amount of money that we all know he doesn't have to pay for the meal, insisting he was sorry for ruining everyone's night." Sean finally looked at Gavin, this time with an apologetic frown. "Tell him I'm sorry and that I had a great time. Dinner is on me."

"Are you sure?" Gavin wanted to hug his friend.

Sean just nodded and patted Gavin's shoulder. "Just go to him. He was so embarrassed, Gav. I'll handle this."

Before he left, Gavin shot his harshest glare at Nate. "He may handle this tonight, but I promise you have not heard the last from me about this." With that, he turned on his heel and headed out to find Davy.

When Gavin made it to his truck in the parking lot, he found Davy leaning against the fender, and Mason speaking calmly to him with his hand on Davy's shoulder. Gavin sidled up to Davy and hooked a finger through a belt loop on Davy's jeans. Davy looked so good tonight in a bright-blue polo and what Gavin knew he considered his best pair of dark-blue jeans. Why had Nate fucked up the night? Davy had seemed to really be in his element all night, and that was something Gavin had worked hard to create for him with the guys.

Gavin pulled Davy to him by the belt loop. "Hey, you." He nuzzled in the spot behind Davy's ear that he knew drove Davy nuts.

Davy flinched away from the contact. Gavin turned to Mason, who shook his head sadly. "Thanks, Mase. I got him."

Mason patted Davy's cheek. "We had a great time, dude. I'll see you for lunch next week. Cool?"

Davy stared at the ground, silently chewing his bottom lip. Gavin could tell he was holding back tears. It broke Gavin's heart. Gavin waited for Mason to leave before he pulled a rigid Davy into a fierce hug.

"I'm sorry about Nate, Davy. I know he can be a bitch. I don't know what he said, but I'm sorry."

Davy pushed him away. Gavin could have been stabbed in that moment and it would have hurt less. He grabbed Davy's hand and used his other to lift Davy's chin. "Look at me, babe." Gavin didn't even stop himself from using the endearment.

Davy chewed his bottom lip for a moment, then looked at Gavin. As soon as their gazes met, Davy's eyes filled with tears and his face went bright red.

"Hey, hey. Don't be like that. It's cool."

"I'm sorry, Gavin. I'm such a freak." Davy said it so quietly Gavin almost missed it.

"Stop that. Everyone had a great time." Gavin stopped one of Davy's falling tears with a swipe of his thumb. "What'd he say to you?"

"Nothing. It's stupid. I'm just socially inept. A spine would help." Davy tried to look away again, but Gavin made him hold the gaze.

"You are funny and smart, and everyone thinks you're great. So stop thinking so little of yourself. We had an awesome time. I don't know what got into Nate."

"He thinks I'm a 'plaything.'" Davy used air quotes, so Gavin assumed that was a direct quote.

"Say what, now?"

"He wondered out loud when the 'plaything,' otherwise known as me, was going to stop being included. He was sure you were tired of playing doting boyfriend just to 'get some ass.'" More air quotes.

Gavin wanted to roll his eyes because it was a ridiculous thing to say. What was this, eighth grade?

"Do you even hear that? It sounds completely ridiculous. And you've said yourself, no one *makes* Gavin Walker do anything, even play boyfriend for a piece of ass."

"I know that." Davy's blush extended to his ears.

Gavin knew it was wrong to think it, but dammit, it was cute.

"Well, then what's the problem?" Gavin kissed Davy's forehead.

"My ex, hell all three of my exes, their friends said shit like that, and it was true. Guys use me, Gav. It's what they do. I'm shy and I'm weird, so I thought I was lucky to have someone around even if it meant I had to stick with an asshole who only kept me around for an easy lay until he found something better."

Oh, Davy.

Gavin placed his lips to Davy's, putting as much emotion into the kiss as he could without getting carried away. He hoped it was comforting. When he pulled away, he said, "You said to me once that you didn't know who'd convinced me I wasn't good enough, and I'm saying that I get who did it to you, but you're more than good enough. You're better than I deserve, Davy." Davy shook his head but Gavin scowled. "Stop. You are. You're fucking amazing and I love you. You're not some fucking plaything. You're so special to me."

Yeah. He'd said it. Not exactly how he'd intended to drop the L word. And Davy was obviously not expecting it, judging by his wide eyes.

"That's right, Davy. I don't know what you did to me." Gavin laughed and took Davy's face in his hands. "I love you, Davy Cooper."

Davy blinked.

Blinked again.

"I love you too," Davy said with a shaky voice.

Gavin let out a breath he didn't realize he'd been holding. A part of him knew Davy loved him too. But hearing the words come out of that beautiful mouth was just amazing, life affirming. Yeah. Perfect phrasing, that. Gavin felt so fucking alive with Davy. He decided to prove it. He grabbed him by the nape of his neck and pulled him into a fierce, hot kiss. As Gavin slipped his tongue through Davy's lips, Davy let out a needy sob. Gavin tilted his head and licked as deep into Davy's mouth as he could. Their bodies came together, Davy's fists clutching Gavin's chest. Gavin realized with a start just how close he was to coming in his pants when Davy's hard cock rubbed against his leg.

He pulled away, staring lustfully at Davy's face. Davy's eyes were wild with need, lips red and shiny-wet from kissing. "We can't do this here. Let's go home," Gavin panted.

Home. Gavin realized how right it felt to think of home as wherever Davy was. Everything with Davy was always so right. Davy peeked around, obviously scanning to see if they'd been seen making out in the parking lot. Then he groaned and buried his face in the nook where Gavin's neck and shoulder met.

Gavin almost asked what was wrong now until he noticed Sean and Mason giving a thumbs-up through the window of the restaurant and Devon making obscene dry-humping motions.

Idiots.

CHAPTER FOURTEEN

GAVIN DROVE to his house since it was closer to the restaurant. Davy was quiet, but didn't seem as freaked out as he had earlier. Davy had Gavin's hand clasped on the armrest. He wanted so much to just enjoy the moment, let it soak in and warm him. He refused to let Nate being a total douche bag fuck up the night he'd finally told Davy he loved him.

And Davy said it back.

Gavin's heart was beating like a hummingbird. He just knew it was trying to fly out through his throat. That would explain why he was so choked up. He'd never dreamed that he'd find someone who made him feel like Davy did. After all of Gavin's fuckups in the beginning, he sure as hell wasn't going to let his dumbass friend fuck up something so good. And Davy was the best thing he'd had in a long time. His friends were great, but Davy was… hope. Davy was hope. And love. And Davy made him feel peace. That was the only thing that could explain why he had no problem accepting that he wanted Davy and he wanted him always.

Well. That was a conversation for another day. Right now, Gavin's only thought was getting Davy home to prove just how much he loved him and how much Gavin wanted to be with him.

Gavin pulled the truck into the driveway of his house and made quick work of hustling Davy in through the private door to his suite. By the time they'd stumbled into the bedroom, Gavin was all hands and Davy was laughing so fucking sweetly that Gavin wanted to burst. Gavin was so happy he could make Davy smile. He thought that was the best talent God had given him. Who needed to know how to play a guitar when you could get Davy to laugh that amazing laugh that bubbled up from such a genuine place inside that wonderful soul?

Gavin still wasn't sure when he'd started waxing lyrical over him.

"What?" Davy asked, obviously laughing at him.

Gavin couldn't respond. Gavin had told the man he loved him, but the rest of it seemed like entirely too much vulnerability. He was scared. But this was Davy. That seemed to be enough for his brain whenever he started freaking out lately. He just had to tell himself, *this is Davy*, and the band of anxiety that had started constricting his heart would ease enough for him to spring into action. Gavin didn't want to think too much on how that could be just as much a bad thing as a good one. The old saying "If someone has the ability to sweep you off your feet, they have the ability to drop you on your ass" tried to edge its way in sometimes. But he couldn't let it. He couldn't afford to.

He wouldn't let his mom or Max win anymore.

Gavin smiled back at Davy. He searched Davy's amused face that was still a bit puffy from crying earlier. "You know I wasn't fucking around when I told you that I love you, right?"

Davy's features reddened and he looked down.

"Davy, don't. I'm here. You're here. We both want to be with each other and we love each other. I love you."

"I love you too. I don't know how, but I do," Davy said quietly.

Gavin held his gaze fiercely. "I don't know why you gave me a chance with your heart, honestly. But I want to be worthy of it."

Davy was silent for a minute, and then he smiled timidly. That tether that had been theoretical between them made itself known, pulling Gavin to him. Gavin dropped his head down to slide his lips over Davy's, and Davy let out another one of his quiet sobs, but this time there were no tears, just need. They started fumbling with each other's clothes. Their shirts fell to the floor, pants and shoes kicked to the side as they tumbled on the bed together.

Gavin ran his hands over the smooth planes of Davy's flat belly, soaking in the warmth and nearness of his lover. As he grazed his fingers over Davy's nipples, Davy's breath hitched. Gavin smiled wickedly into their kiss and lowered his hand down to Davy's swollen cock, which was leaking and ready. Davy let out the sweetest fucking whimper, goading Gavin on. Gavin's own cock was desperate for friction as he rubbed it against Davy's solid thigh.

Gavin started pulling Davy's cock, stroking roughly and grunting into his mouth as he rutted their bodies together. Davy was panting and wild beneath him. Gavin was high with the feeling of driving his shy lover into total abandon.

Gavin shuddered when Davy cupped Gavin's balls and gently massaged them in their sensitive sac. He moved his leg, giving Davy a better angle, better friction as Gavin's cock found the crevice between Davy's cock and thigh. Gavin hunched his back into a thorough scraping of Davy's nails down his spine. Gavin's senses flared to life as Davy became wilder and more uninhibited in their coupling.

Gavin gripped Davy's ass with his free hand and pulled Davy's hip up to meet each of his thrusts. Davy moved his hands to the sensitive skin behind Gavin's balls and using two fingers, he rubbed it firmly. Gavin bit into the muscle between Davy's neck and shoulder, earning a sexy groan from Davy. Gavin watched as he licked his own full, pouty lips, pink tongue darting out to drive Gavin insane.

Gavin released the firm globe of Davy's ass and eased his fingers into the crack, finding Davy's hole. He sank the tip of his pointer finger into Davy's heat. "Gavin. Oh, fuck, Gavin," Davy said on a moan. "So good."

Davy, following Gavin's lead, moved his hand farther back to Gavin's hole and fingered the sensitive muscle. They met for a hard, bruising kiss that Gavin was surprised Davy was capable of. Both men rocked onto the other's finger, going deeper with each downward push. Gavin crooked his finger.

"Goddamn, Gavin! So fucking good," Davy growled.

Fucking *growled*. That was one helluva pleasant surprise and probably the sexiest thing Gavin had ever heard.

Gavin separated from the kiss and moved on top of Davy, keeping his legs open wide so they could both still fuck each other with fingers while Gavin lined their cocks up and fisted them together. Gavin leaned his entire upper body against Davy's. He kissed and nipped along Davy's shoulder, then lining them both up just right, began a rough thrusting. They both fucked Gavin's fist with a forward motion, then fell back onto invading digits. Gavin felt the power of Davy's body beneath him, the humming underneath the skin. The way their skin touched, their cocks and balls gliding together made Gavin's mind reel. He didn't understand how he could feel so connected to one person without one of them being inside the other, but this was so much. This was overwhelming.

"Come for me, Davy. Let go."

Davy stilled, regaining some of the guardedness in his eyes and quietly said, "It's scary to let go."

Gavin's chest tightened. He wanted to refute that, but he couldn't. Fuck yes, it was horrifying. He knew what it meant to be scared, to be alone. All he had was a promise, his words. "You're never alone again, okay. It's you and me."

Gavin ran his knuckles gently over Davy's cheek, trying to soothe. "I'll jump if you jump." He knew it was lame, but his mind was short-circuiting with all the love and the sweaty skin and the smell of man. His chest was so close to Davy's, Gavin couldn't tell if it was his heart beating so fast or if it was Davy's. All he knew was that they both beat and they were both there.

Gavin started moving again. "Let go, babe." He leaned in and kissed the spot behind Davy's ear that drove Davy wild.

One, two, three thrusts. "Fuck, Gavin." Davy made the sweetest sound of surrender as his come erupted from his cock and painted their bellies, their cocks.

Gavin threw his head back as the come made the warm glide of their cocks smoother and oh so dirty. "I love you. God, I love you, Davy." And Gavin really meant it. His own orgasm barreled over him, blinding him and making a joyous laugh join his moan as his own come joined Davy's on their skin.

Gavin kissed Davy with lips, tongue, and the taste of sweat. The kiss wasn't hurried or done to arouse, just basking in the afterglow. Gavin was sated and felt strong with Davy wrapped around him. He never realized how strong or reliable he could really feel until he had to be reliable for Ray and for Davy. And these days he was feeling as though he could do anything as long as Davy was willing to be there, scared as hell and stumbling just the same as Gavin, but there all the same.

THEY HAD both dozed off quickly after they'd finished another round of lovemaking. Davy was the first to wake the next morning and lay there for a while watching Gavin. To see Gavin relaxed and vulnerable made him look his twenty-two years. Usually, the man carried enough weight on his shoulders that he looked older and worn-down. But Davy noticed that more and more lately, Gavin was looking as young awake as he did sleeping when they were together, just the two of them.

Gavin was incredible, opening his heart that had been ripped out and fed to him by his first love and his own mother. When Gavin told Davy he loved him, Davy had gone weak. He had been feeling it, but was scared enough of running Gavin off that he'd kept it inside. Hell, Gavin freaked out over having feelings for Davy, so Davy just knew the L word would be a deal breaker. So when Gavin said it first, it had taken Herculean effort not to fall over in the parking lot.

And when was Davy able to let go of his mother's weird social conditioning and not flip out over one guy's snarky bullshit? He knew as soon as he'd arrived at the restaurant that Nate wasn't happy to see him, but what else was new? Everyone said Nate was just bitchy, but he seemed to have it in for Davy. Although Davy could be imagining that. He still sucked with social cues. Could be that he just couldn't handle snarky jokes, though he was pretty sure with the way everyone reacted that they hadn't been jokes.

Damn if Davy didn't hate his social ineptitude. It made dating Gavin awkward, since Gavin was a social creature. Davy felt guilty any time Gavin declined an offer to go out in favor of sitting around while Davy did homework, or got carryout rather than going to dinner with friends.

110

After their first road bumps, despite the guy's reputation, Gavin turned out to be a solid guy. He still had his moments—he was still a bit of an asshole—but no one was perfect.

Davy scooted closer to Gavin, laid his head on Gavin's shoulder, and hooked an arm around his naked waist. Davy kept his hips away from Gavin's body, his morning erection raging at the nearness of all that nakedness—Gavin's nakedness. He resisted the urge to lick around the tattoos on Gavin's chest. Gavin looked so tired lately. This was the latest Davy had known either of them to sleep in in a while, so he didn't want to wake Gavin until it was absolutely necessary.

Apparently Gavin was already awake, though, because he wrapped the arm Davy was lying on around Davy's back and grabbed Davy's ass, then pulled him against his side. Davy closed his eyes and hissed as his cock made contact with Gavin's hairy thigh. It was a delicious sensation, and Davy's balls drew up, threatening to end any hope of further morning fun. He closed his eyes and let himself enjoy just feeling every sensation.

"Mmmm," Gavin mumbled. His voice was sleep roughened and deep. Damn, it was sexy. Davy opened his eyes to see Gavin looking at him with open lust, which was even sexier with sleep-swollen features and bedhead. Davy moved the hand he had wrapped around Gavin's waist to cup Gavin's heavy balls. Gavin arched into his touch. Davy smiled and kissed Gavin's shoulder, jaw, then cheek.

Gavin turned his head to capture Davy's mouth with his. It wasn't rough, just a lazy morning kiss with a hint of arousal and full of welcoming affection. The kiss didn't last long. Gavin pushed Davy on his back and rolled on top of him. Davy stopped Gavin's rutting, wrapping his arms around Gavin's lower back and hugging them together tightly. Gavin stilled as Davy burrowed into his chest, placing gentle kisses on his throat. Davy just wanted to hold him close for a minute and for a second thought Gavin might break the embrace. He let out a contented sigh as Gavin relaxed into him, wrapping his arms around Davy's shoulders and holding him tightly.

Davy smiled against Gavin's shoulder, enjoying the smell of Gavin's skin and the pleasant scent drifting from the sheets that smelled of them together. Davy had never felt as content as he did now, safely hidden from the world in the bubble that was him and Gavin together, embracing, skin-to-skin.

Gavin tugged Davy's hair, pulling Davy's head back gently. He had the sexiest grin spread across his face. Davy wondered how he'd ever found that cocky bastard annoying. Right now, just the hot breath gusting across his cheek shot electric thrills straight to his cock.

Gavin leaned down and kissed Davy on the lips, then his chin. From there, Gavin licked a blazing-hot line to Davy's Adam's apple where he started licking in swirls and sucking. Davy never thought he'd be turned on just from having someone suck on his Adam's apple, but Gavin's tongue was so skilled that every swirl felt like a twist on the head of Davy's cock. Davy's hips canted up involuntarily and Gavin sat up, looking pleased with himself.

"I'm gonna suck you," Gavin said very matter-of-factly.

"Okay." Davy barely got the words out around the lust clogging his throat. He found his voice enough to say, "I want to suck you too."

Gavin's nostrils flared. That obviously pleased him. He nodded, chest heaving with every heavy breath as he ran a thumb over Davy's bottom lip in a way that raised goose bumps over Davy's whole body. Davy reached up and traced the single sparrow tattooed on Gavin's left pec. He sucked Gavin's thumb into his mouth and bit it lightly. Gavin stared at him through half-lidded eyes. Davy moved his fingers down from the tattoo and pinched Gavin's nipple. Gavin closed his eyes, sighing at the contact. Davy patted Gavin's hip, impatient to taste him again.

He found that his thoughts often turned to the taste of Gavin in his mouth. Gavin's tongue, Gavin's skin, Gavin's cock. Davy had never been so addicted to something as he was to the taste of Gavin. The thought of anyone else ever having tasted him burned him to the core with jealousy. It was almost enough to make him tie Gavin up in his apartment and keep him around forever. Just so no one else would ever have *this*, what they were doing now, with Gavin ever again. He wasn't sure when he'd become so fucking possessive.

When Gavin turned, offering his proud, lovely cock, Davy sucked it down greedily, not hesitating to take it right into his throat, getting a pleased "Fuuuuuuck" from Gavin. If Davy could have managed a smile, he would have, but Gavin's girth wouldn't allow it. Davy sucked and used his throat muscles to work Gavin's cock and hummed his satisfaction when Gavin took him into the wet heat of his mouth. They started fucking each other's mouths in earnest. Gavin kneaded Davy's ass with his long, elegant fingers. Davy came off Gavin's cock with a sucking pop and gave a moan before laving Gavin's balls, swirling each of them around in figure eights.

Davy inhaled the musk of Gavin's arousal, and his own cock throbbed and swelled in Gavin's expert mouth. Gavin swirled his tongue around the crown of Davy's cock and applied a strong suction just to the head, using his lips to create a steady friction that had Davy squirming. Davy used his hands to part Gavin's asscheeks. Gavin had the most beautiful ass Davy had ever seen. Two perfect, round globes that were meaty and firm, the kind of ass that looked good no matter how baggy the pants Gavin wore.

Davy licked in circles, making a path with his tongue from Gavin's taint to his entrance. Davy spit on Gavin's hole, then licked the wetted muscle, lapping and jabbing until it yielded enough that the tip of his tongue slipped in a fraction. Gavin pushed his ass back into Davy's face. This time Davy could smile at Gavin's reaction, and he did.

Gavin stopped sucking for a moment, just stroking Davy's cock and rocking back into the thorough rim job Davy was giving him. Davy eased his hand into the mix, massaged Gavin's taint with his forefingers, and pushed his thumb into Gavin's entrance.

"Davy. Don't stop, baby. So good. You drive me wild," Gavin said through what sounded like gritted teeth. Gavin started grinding his cock on Davy's chest, then took Davy back into his mouth and sucked with a vengeance.

He continued fingering Gavin in all his most sensitive areas.

Lust took Davy over completely as he began fucking Gavin's throat with sharp upward jabs. Gavin just kept grinding down and back on him. Davy delivered a hard smack to Gavin's meaty ass, and Gavin moaned from somewhere deep inside, the vibrations bringing Davy's orgasm on him full force.

"Fuck, Gav. I'm coming. Fuck. I'm coming!" Davy yelled. Gavin didn't let up, just kept sucking hard. Davy kept sinking his thumb into him, the heat goading his orgasm on as he emptied his balls down Gavin's throat. Davy couldn't stop the loud "Holy shit!" he hollered. He kept up his ministrations with his hands through the spasms of his body until Gavin went stiff, mashing his cock so hard on Davy's chest it had to hurt, then shot thick ropes of creamy come.

Before Davy could wrap his mind around it, Gavin flipped himself around and started licking his come off Davy's chest, every once in a while catching a nipple with his tongue. Davy stared at Gavin as he licked his own come from his lips, then moved in for a salty kiss. Davy carded his fingers through Gavin's soft hair, reveling in the taste of them together. The taste of their kiss and their come commingling. It was the most erotic, intimate moment of Davy's life and he never wanted it to end.

Until the alarm went off.

"Dammit," Davy complained.

Gavin looked down at him, eyes still half-lidded, mouth stretched and red from the brutal fucking it had received. Gavin stretched over to the bedside table to shut off the alarm, then turned breathlessly to Davy. "We are so doing that shit again."

A laugh burst out of Davy that he continued all the way to the shower. God, he loved that man.

CHAPTER FIFTEEN

THE FOLLOWING Thursday dawned bright and sunny, but as was common no matter the time of year in Seattle, the sky had gone gray and overcast by midday with light sprinkles misting enough to make the people walking on the sidewalk outside the shop open their umbrellas. Davy's day had been entirely too slow for his liking. For the tourist-heavy month of June, he'd seen no one out at the market, and the water-view park across the street was empty save for a few random homeless people camping out on the picnic tables under the pavilion.

The rustle of pages being turned took Davy's attention from the outside world, and he chose to focus instead on his sexy boyfriend, who was doing homework in a corner booth. Gavin had started spending even more time with him. Davy had mentioned to Gavin that he felt bad sucking him into Davy's hermit lifestyle, but Gavin brushed it off, saying maybe he'd outgrown the need to constantly go out. Davy wasn't convinced, but it was nice to see Gavin deep in thought over his Art History textbook, there if Davy wanted a quick kiss or to sit with him on a break.

Davy looked up at the clock to see it was a quarter 'til four. "Hey, Gav," Davy said. Gavin looked up from his work. "Henry said I could close up at four since it's slow." It wasn't unusual for them to close early on slow days, and Davy wasn't complaining. He could live without working his scheduled double that would have lasted until nine. He was more than eager to get out of the shop and spend some time with Gavin that might include kissing and tongues and groping.

"Need help?" Gavin asked, pulling Davy out of his dirty thoughts. Gavin smiled at him knowingly.

Davy cleared his throat. "If you'll lock the door and switch off the open sign, I'll finish up back here. Shouldn't take long." Since it hadn't gotten very busy that day, Davy didn't have any cleanup other than the few tins he'd used to make shakes for a group of elderly tourists earlier in the day.

After washing the tins, Davy came around the counter with the broom to sweep under the tables.

"Hey!" Gavin yelled, startling him.

Davy turned, wide-eyed, to him. "What the hell?"

"I love this song." Gavin pointed at the speaker hanging in the corner.

Davy so often tuned out the oldies station that he hadn't noticed what was playing. "*You* like Aretha Franklin?" Davy looked at him incredulously. Usually in Gavin's truck Gavin played rap or indie rock bands that Davy had never heard of.

Gavin grabbed the broom from Davy and threw it in a corner, then pulled Davy by the hand to the middle of the room. "What can I say? I'm full of surprises."

That was for damn sure. And an even bigger surprise was when Gavin started belting the words to "Hooked on Your Love" with Aretha. "Hooked on your love, sweet lovin'…," Gavin sang.

Davy blinked. He wasn't sure why he was surprised. He guessed it would make sense for Gavin to be into older music with his love for all things "old-school." But Motown? Davy laughed as Gavin put him into a spin, then pulled him back against him, clasping him tight and grinding their hips together.

Davy was mesmerized by Gavin's golden singing voice. He could have sworn he'd heard him sing before, so how had he not noticed that rich baritone? Even though he was being completely silly, Gavin still sang the song beautifully. This time Gavin separated them and spun under their joined arms, then came back to Davy, ass to Davy's crotch, as he swayed them. Davy laughed at Gavin's sweet abandon as they danced together.

By the end of the song, they were both laughing and Davy was feeling light as air. Davy stopped, completely taken with the joy on Gavin's face. Gavin smiled so serenely at him, eyes full of happiness. "God, I'm so in love with you, Davy Cooper."

Davy blushed, but smiled back. His heart was so light in that moment. It was such a sweet feeling.

Gavin kissed him, then held him close as they rocked to a slower Nat King Cole song. Gavin's arms felt so strong and sure around his waist. Davy was finding it harder and harder to pick a favorite of his moments with Gavin, but he knew this one would rank right up at the top.

After a while of swaying and a few slow kisses, getting lost in their bubble, they started becoming impatient, and Davy could feel Gavin's hardness against his thigh. Davy regretfully pulled out of the embrace.

"Okay, I gotta finish up," he said, trying to be the voice of reason, though he really didn't want to. He laughed at Gavin when Gavin poked out his bottom lip in a pout. "You're ridiculous." God, he loved how comfortable he was with Gavin. He'd never felt so free or open around someone. "We're just lucky I already clocked out. It'll take five minutes to finish up."

Gavin huffed in mock annoyance. "Fine. I'll pack up my stuff."

Davy made his way back around the corner, and Gavin stomped over to the booth he'd been sitting at to pack his book away in his messenger bag, every once in a while throwing a pouty look over his shoulder at Davy like a petulant child.

"Pitiful. You're effing pitiful, Gavin."

"But you love me."

Gavin smiled brightly, almost looking like the happy child he'd never had the chance to be. It stilled Davy's heart.

"Yes, I do love you," Davy said, shaking his head. "Though I don't know why."

"Hey!" Gavin said in mock offense.

Davy just waved him off. "Stop distracting me so I can make Ray his to-go peanut butter shake, then we can go home and screw our brains out." He couldn't tell who was more surprised by his statement. He didn't say stuff like that. What had Gavin done to him? Gavin obviously was enjoying this new Davy, though, because he let out a shocked guffaw.

Gavin came to the counter and leaned over to where Davy was counting down his cash drawer, then stole a kiss. "That sounds fucking awesome." Davy felt his face heat under Gavin's leer. "Although, I don't know who'll be happier. I mean as much as I enjoy sex, especially sex with you, I think if he was a few years younger, Ray would marry you just for your peanut butter shakes."

Davy pulled out his most seductive look, damning how silly he felt. "Well, I am pretty good at all things that require a little… sucking."

Gavin's eyes widened and he gripped his heart dramatically. "Damn, baby. You need to hurry the hell up." He reached across and grabbed Davy by the shirt, then pulled him into a sloppy kiss. "I'd like to put that theory to the test."

A full-body shudder wracked Davy. It took him less than five minutes to be out the door.

"RAY, WE'RE home," Gavin called out as he led Davy by his hand into the house.

Davy realized Gavin had been doing things like that more and more lately. Maybe Davy wasn't the only one who felt a little possessive. He didn't mind in the least. Touching Gavin, even in the simple ways, drove him wild and made him feel cared for.

"In the den, Gavin," Ray said to direct them.

Davy set down the to-go cup that held Ray's peanut butter shake and took his hand back from Gavin so they could take their shoes off. When Davy kicked his shoes into the corner where everyone else's were piled, he turned, and Gavin stole a kiss. Davy jumped in surprise, then laughed at himself.

"So jumpy," Gavin teased, poking him in the ribs where he was most ticklish.

"What are you, four years old?" Davy swatted at Gavin's searching hands. "Stop!" He laughed, moving toward the den at a brisk pace, Gavin hot on his trail.

Davy stopped in his tracks, Gavin running into his back, when he saw Ray had company. He didn't really need to ask who she was when Gavin took his hand in his and gripped it as if he might float out to sea if he let go.

The woman was an older, feminine version of Gavin. She was tall and thin with the same deep-brown eyes, and Davy knew if her eyebrows hadn't been done, they'd have that same prominent shape as Gavin's. Other than her clothes, which would have looked more appropriate on a twenty-year-old, she looked older than he'd expected.

Carmen Walker looked from Gavin to Davy, then at their linked hands. For a moment, Davy thought he saw annoyance in her eyes, but she quickly recovered with a smile that was eerily similar to Gavin's smile when he was feeling contrite—which, let's face it, was rare, and she was no better at contrite than he was.

"Hello, Gavin."

"Carmen." Even Davy flinched at the icy tone Gavin shot at her. If Davy didn't know their past, he would have felt bad for the woman.

"Gavin...." Ray's voice was reproachful.

Davy looked at Gavin, who was staring hard at his mother.

"What's she doing here?"

"Well, my father is sick and my son is dealing with it all on his own," Carmen said, as if it was the stupidest question she'd ever heard.

Gavin scoffed and let go of Davy's hand to stalk over to her space.

"Gavin, back down." Ray tried to ease out of his chair, but his eyes glassed over in pain, so Davy rushed to his side and put a hand on Ray's shoulder, pushing him gently back down into the chair. Carmen shot another look that could be read as annoyed at Davy, but he couldn't say for certain. He really wished he was better with people.

"You expect me to believe you're just here, out of the blue, to help?" Gavin's voice rose with every word.

Carmen held his gaze. "I know you have no reason to trust me, but you don't know the whole story. I'm here to help and to try to be a family. I know I have to prove myself, but I'm here to try."

Davy almost gasped hearing Gavin's mother say words similar to the ones Gavin had once spoken to him. Gavin flinched back, obviously affected. Carmen's eyes flashed in victory, much the same as Gavin's had at one time. Davy was stunned at the resemblance, but he knew that was where their similarities ended. He still had a sense there wasn't much pretty lurking beyond the woman's surface, whereas beyond his hard surface, Gavin was all goodness.

"Fuck this. I won't hear it." Gavin marched over to Davy and snatched him by the hand.

Davy could see the desperate need to flee in his lover, and the pain in Gavin's eyes made him want to pull Gavin close and make everything better, though he knew he couldn't.

"Come on, Davy. We're fucking out of here."

Davy winced. Gavin obviously didn't realize he was still yelling. Even if he did, Gavin was freaking out too much for Davy to think telling him to calm down would be wise. Davy went along as Gavin tugged him toward the door, throwing Ray an apologetic look. Before they made it out, though, Davy froze, pulling Gavin up short. Gavin tried to tug, but Davy stayed rooted to the spot looking at the door to the kitchen and pulled back on Gavin's hand.

"What in the serious *fuck*?" Gavin turned on Davy.

Davy put a hand on Gavin's face and let him have a moment to breathe. Gavin's nostrils flared, gaze darting over Davy's face, wild with the need to run.

"Gavin, you gotta calm down."

"What the fuck for?"

Davy did his best to not shrink under Gavin's anger and panic. "Gav, you're scaring him." Davy nodded toward the young boy who'd come in from the kitchen, wide-eyed and apparently startled from all the

120

yelling. Carmen noticed the boy at the same time Gavin did and moved toward him.

"And who in the fuck is that?" Gavin's voice was so small.

"Language," Carmen scolded. She folded the boy, who couldn't have been more than three or four years old, up in her arms and lifted him onto her hip.

Davy didn't know how Gavin could ask such a silly question. The boy looked at them with another pair of those deep-brown eyes from under that similar noble brow as he hid in his mother's shoulder.

"Who in the *fuck* is that?" Gavin was working himself into a fit.

Davy gripped Gavin's shoulder, awaiting the blow.

"Gavin," Carmen started, smiling at the child. "This is Oliver. Your brother."

CHAPTER SIXTEEN

"*WHAT?*" GAVIN knew he was yelling. Even Davy's steadying hand on his arm wasn't helping him regain control. And Gavin hated losing control. Especially when he did so because of his mother. From the moment he'd seen her face, he'd completely lost his grip.

"Gavin, calm down," Davy said softly.

Gavin felt bad when Davy had to put up an obvious fight not to cower under the glare Gavin shot him. Davy rubbed his arm, trying to comfort him. It wasn't working. Gavin was shaking. He wasn't really angry or scared, his nerves were just completely shot. It was too much to take in.

His mother. Here. Still dressing as though she was Gavin's age, but she had a waistline that spoke of too much beer and a face aged from too many rough nights. He had a flash of sympathy, knowing not all of it was her fault. He'd gone to Al-Anon a few times and knew alcoholism was a disease, but that fact didn't erase a fucked-up childhood. And it sure didn't erase the image of his first love balls-deep in his own mother on the same couch where he'd shared his first kiss with Max—his first kiss ever.

He closed his eyes against the flood of painful memories. Reality sucked right now. No matter how far he'd run from it, it just wouldn't let him go.

Holy shit. And a brother? One who looked so much like him that it created an ache in Gavin's chest. Gavin was sad for not knowing the kid, and he felt horrible because it was plain that he was scaring the shit out of him, and he knew their mother had probably damaged little Oliver enough without Gavin giving the kid a nervous condition. He tried to reel in his emotions, anchoring himself to Davy's touch. Gavin gripped the hand Davy had on his arm and breathed in and out with his eyes closed. Davy murmured quiet reassurances that Gavin appreciated more than he was capable of expressing, especially right then.

"We should take this in the other room. Away from small ears," Ray said. Ray struggled through his pain to try to get out of his easy chair.

Gavin smiled at how quickly Davy let go of his arm to rush to Ray's aid. The fact that Davy knew Gavin would prefer Ray be helped than for Gavin to be coddled went a long way to distracting Gavin enough that he could pull himself together. Watching Ray give in to Davy's kindness, accepting him so completely, was such a stunning thing to Gavin.

"You're right," Gavin said calmly. He walked over to help Davy with Ray's weight.

The old guy laughed and said, "Of course I am."

Gavin and Davy laughed, despite the tension of the moment. Ray started making his way toward the kitchen.

Gavin held out his hand for Davy to come with him. "Davy?"

Gavin almost snapped again when he saw the slightest temper flare in his mother's eyes. Ray held up a hand. "Davy, I'm gonna need something stronger than that peanut butter shake, so why don't you let Oliver there have it? Would you mind watching him for a minute while I take care of these knuckleheads?"

Gavin and Carmen started to protest, Davy looking very unsure at Ray's request.

"Ray. Davy is important to me. He should be there."

Ray shook his head at Gavin in the way he did when he thought Gavin was being a jackass. "No, Gavin, Davy here is important to all of us. He's family. But I'm sure he and Oliver would rather not watch you and your mother box like a pair of drunk kangaroos."

He knew Ray was right. Neither Davy nor Oliver deserved to watch Gavin and Carmen square off. But Ray's acknowledgment of Davy as family created such a heady feeling that Gavin's knees went weak. Gavin looked at Davy, who was chewing his bottom lip but smiling and looking at the floor, before collecting himself and holding his arms out to take Oliver from a dumbfounded Carmen. Gavin wasn't sure what it was to her that Davy was important to them. She didn't know shit about what his relationship was with Davy or with Ray. *Fuck her.*

"C'mon, Ollie. Me and you, we're gonna go look at your brother's model cars. Sound cool?"

Oliver looked uncertainly at his mother, and when she relented, still looking at her father with wide eyes, Oliver smiled and said, "Cars."

Gavin fell in love with one single word. When Davy took Oliver in his arms and said, "Nice to meet you, Ollie," Gavin thought he'd seen God when Davy used the nickname, and he and Oliver smiled at each other.

"I'm not Ollie, I'm Oliver!" Oliver said enthusiastically in the way only a kid could.

Davy shook his head. "Oh, no. I'm calling you Ollie. 'Cuz I'm too lazy to say Oliver."

Oliver laughed at Davy and said, "Silly."

Gavin couldn't recall ever having been such a happy child. He wondered with some envy whether Carmen was actually a loving mother for Oliver or whether he was just a resilient child. *He's probably like one of those third-world orphans who don't get enough love, so they cling to everyone else really easily.* Gavin laughed sardonically at his cynical inner voice.

"Is that settled?" Ray asked. He was clearly as pleased as Gavin was at the sight of Davy and Oliver's interaction, as his face was full of pure affection. God, Gavin was thinking he'd turned into total mush on the inside. Damn that Davy. And now the kid? Davy and Oliver chose that moment to look at Gavin with wide eyes and bright smiles.

He was so screwed.

Gavin scowled at Carmen, who was still looking over the scene with a mix of wonderment and what Gavin still considered too much like annoyance. That only served to get him hot under the collar all over again. "Let's get this over with," he snapped.

Carmen and Ray both frowned at him but they headed into the kitchen. He looked at Davy, who gave him a reassuring half-smile, and then Gavin followed his grandfather and his erstwhile mother into a room that had been his safest place for so long. And he couldn't help but be furious because here she was. She was taking the walls down on his safe place, replacing them with the mold and the rot that were his painful memories with her.

Stop being so dramatic, he scolded himself.

"Okay, Carmen. I'm waiting," Gavin said, watching her help Ray ease into his chair at the breakfast table.

She looked around the room for a moment. "Wow, the memories in this old house...." She looked as though she was reflecting on the room fondly, though she'd done nothing but trash her memories of the place she'd grown up and her childhood for as long as Gavin could remember.

"I'm not here for you to reminisce about your past, which last time I checked you weren't so fond of." Gavin saw that Ray was not pleased with his bitchy tone. He couldn't help himself, though. He didn't trust the woman as far as he could throw her. "Why. Are. You. Here?" He bit each word off, looking at Carmen pointedly.

She stood, squaring her shoulders. "I wanted you to meet your brother and for your grandfather to have a chance to know Oliver before he died."

"But why now, Carmen?" Ray asked. "Not that I'm not grateful to see the boy, I just don't understand the timing. I've been sick a long time."

Carmen went to speak, but Gavin cut her off. "Or you could have brought him years ago when Ray wasn't sick. I mean, how old is the kid anyways? Three? Four?"

"He just turned three in March."

Carmen was a bit shamefaced at the answer. Gavin wondered why, and then he stopped himself from reeling back when he did the math on some things.

"*Why are you here?*" Gavin snarled.

125

"I just finished rehab. Six months sober." She was looking at Ray now. "I heard how sick you were and knew it was time to see you." She looked at Gavin straight on. "Time to come home."

"This is—" Gavin started, but Ray quieted him with a stony gaze.

"This is always your home, Carmen," Ray said calmly.

"What?" Gavin asked incredulously.

"Gavin. I'm disappointed. She's come to make amends. Now, I don't know the whole story of what's gone on between the two of you, and I'm afraid I don't want to know." Ray turned that stony gaze to his daughter. "Carmen, of course you and that boy are welcome here as long as you need. But make no mistake—I don't trust you yet. God knows I love you. You're my baby girl, and I've wanted nothing but to see you standing here in front of me, sober and healthy, for a long time. I feel blessed to have seen it before I die. But this is more for Oliver than for you. He has a right to know his brother."

"Yes, sir." Carmen actually sounded contrite.

"Ray?" Gavin heard the desperation in his own voice.

Carmen walked over to him. "Gavin, I know I did horrible things to you. I do. I'll regret them until the day I die, but I do want to try to make up for it. I want to be here for you so you're not doing this all alone."

Gavin's chin jutted out stubbornly. "I'm not alone. I have Davy."

"Yes. Davy. He seems like a sweet kid."

Gavin could tell Carmen's smile was fake. Or it could be he was just that distrustful of her. And why shouldn't he be?

"Carmen, you'll remember that Davy has been a big help. He's welcome whenever he likes," Ray said, and with that, the subject was closed.

Carmen nodded at her father. "As it should be." She looked back at Gavin. "You obviously care for him." Another fake smile. Or maybe that was her genuine smile. Her face had become tired over the years. Maybe it wasn't capable of a genuinely happy expression.

126

"Can we at least try? If for nothing else, then for your grandfather and for Oliver? Maybe along the way you can learn to trust me again. I'd love to earn your trust again."

Gavin saw some sincerity in her eyes. He sighed, running his fingers through his hair. He looked between Carmen and Ray briefly, then remembered the smiling face of the little brother he'd not known until today. He also imagined what Davy's advice would be. *Davy.* He had Davy. He supposed even if things turned out bad, as he suspected they would, he at least had Davy. And Ray. And he'd always wanted a brother.

"Okay. For Ray. And for Oliver. But"—he kept his arms crossed over his chest and laid his most threatening glare on Carmen—"you will be kind to Davy. I love him." Her eyes widened a fraction, but she didn't respond otherwise.

"Carmen?" Ray nudged.

"Of course, of course." Carmen waved it off as though they were being silly. "My baby's in love. Every mother dreams to hear that."

"Yeah, well, this one won't turn out like the last one I loved. I can promise you that." Gavin watched as the color drained from Carmen's face. "I'm going to find Davy and Oliver." He looked at Ray and got a nod of acknowledgment, then turned on his heel.

"Oh," he said over his shoulder, "I'll stay at Davy's. You and Oliver can have my suite."

"Oh, I wouldn't want to put you out," Carmen said, nose turned up a bit in distaste.

He laughed. "Don't worry. The sheets are clean." He sauntered out of the kitchen, letting the swinging door fly shut behind him.

DAVY WAS in awe as he watched Oliver play with the cars. Davy had given him a couple of the ones Gavin would roll around when he didn't realize Davy could see him playing like a child. Oliver was unusually careful for such a young child. He treated the cars with such reverence, you'd imagine he understood just how much they meant to his brother—or that he'd been sent to obedience school.

Davy tried not to think the worst of Carmen Walker. For Oliver to be as open with Davy as he had been once he'd gotten used to him, Davy couldn't imagine she'd treated him unkindly. He seemed well adjusted. But Davy had never been around kids other than the ones he'd waited on at Bart's, so he could be way off base.

In fact, Davy was probably way more uncomfortable with Ollie than the other way around. He was really out of his element. He may have issues with being around people his own age, but at least he had some experience with them. Children.... He'd never even considered having kids because for one, he didn't figure it'd be something he could do being gay and all, and quite frankly they made him nervous as hell.

He hadn't wanted to disappoint Ray after Ray said such a kind thing, including him as family. He'd gotten choked up when Ray said that. He knew it was too soon. He and Gavin hadn't been together that long. But Davy hadn't had any family other than his uncle for so long that hearing someone considered him as such made him feel like a needy child who wanted to cling to Ray's side and stay there. He wanted to soak in Ray's affection as long as he could. But Davy knew Ray was right. Gavin and his mother needed to sort this out away from Ollie.

"Davy, you like car?" Ollie held out one of the model cars.

Davy smiled at him and moved over to where Ollie played on the bed. "I love them. Not as much as your brother, though. He built these."

Oliver's guileless eyes were full of awe as he said, "Wow," and patted the car as though it was a favorite pet. "Gavvy build the car?" Davy watched Ollie unblinkingly for a moment, the child looking freakishly like a miniature version of Gavin, regardless of whether they had different fathers or not.

Davy shook out of his thoughts as he realized Ollie was looking at him expectantly. "Yep, Ollie. Gavin built this."

"Mommy said Gavvy smart," Ollie said proudly.

"He is. Very smart." Davy watched Ollie warmly. He was so full of love for this kid. How had it happened so quickly? Even with the awkwardness in the beginning, he couldn't help but fall for the kid's charms. *Just like your brother.* Davy mussed Ollie's hair. Ollie surprised him thoroughly by doing something so much like his brother that it hurt.

"Don't do that, Davy!" Ollie fixed his hair, rubbing down the tufts Davy had misplaced.

Davy had watched Gavin do the same thing many times before, been fussed at several times for the same reason. He was so surprised at the mini-Gavin that he started laughing. Ollie looked at him as though he was completely insane. Maybe he was.

Ollie's face became very solemn. "Was Gavvy mad at me?"

Davy was so surprised by the non sequitur that he almost didn't know how to respond for a second. "What? Why?"

Ollie rolled the wheels on a model classic Mustang, sadly watching the turning tires. "Mommy said Gavvy isn't happy with her. Is he mad at me? He was yelling lots."

Davy's chest swelled. "Oh, no. No, no, Ollie. Gavin was just stressed. He was surprised to see your mom. But he loves you, a lot."

Ollie looked up at Davy, still seemingly unconvinced.

Davy smiled reassuringly. "In fact, I bet he's got all kinds of fun stuff he's going to do with you. I'm sure you could even talk him into letting you help build one of these cars."

Oliver's eyes gleamed. "Really?"

"I'm positive. Your brother is the best."

Ollie nodded.

"What are you two doing down here?" Gavin asked, coming up behind Davy and wrapping an arm around his waist, squeezing tight, and placing his chin on Davy's shoulder.

Ollie studied them curiously, enough to make Davy want to pull away from the embrace. Then Ollie did what children often do. He turned his attention to something else. Davy laughed at himself.

Gavin kissed behind Davy's ear and Davy squeezed Gavin's hand that was on his hip.

"Davy said we can build a car!"

129

Gavin huffed in Davy's ear. "He did, did he?"

"Hey, I'd do anything to keep that kid off my back," Davy mumbled.

"I think, between the two of you, I'm screwed," Gavin said with a put-upon sigh.

"My thoughts exactly," Davy said solemnly, receiving a playful bite on the shoulder in response.

CHAPTER SEVENTEEN

GAVIN ROSE above Davy. Sweat dripped from his brow as their limbs tangled together. They'd gone back to Davy's apartment for the night so Gavin could clear his head, and he'd also given up his suite to his mother and little brother. As soon as they'd gotten in the door, Gavin had clung to Davy and begged Davy to help him think about anything other than their day.

Davy couldn't imagine what Gavin must be feeling. His mom back, a new brother out of thin air. Even Davy was overwhelmed with all of the emotion. Aside from getting angry, Gavin had been so composed once he'd had his talk with Carmen. He'd eventually made nervous attempts to bond with Oliver. Davy had been worried about Gavin, though, as he'd retreated within himself on the drive to Davy's apartment.

But that ended as soon as the lock slid into place on Davy's apartment door. Gavin was feral, searching, desperate as they stripped off their clothes. Davy had been more than happy to oblige as Gavin took his lips with his own. The kiss had been full of need. Gavin, again, felt as though he was holding on to Davy to keep from drifting out to sea and being taken under the rip currents.

Davy rolled on top of him. "Let me take care of you," he said roughly.

Gavin's lust-filled eyes bored into his. He responded with a thrust of his hips into Davy's and a nod. "Please, Davy. Please, please."

Davy couldn't remember him ever having pleaded. Gavin was usually well in control of himself, even on the brink of release. Not tonight, though. Gavin was wild, squirming, and full of pent-up need and energy. Davy moved in for a kiss, and Gavin slithered his tongue into Davy's mouth, forcing his tongue as far in as he could go. Davy ground his cock into Gavin's. Gavin was weeping with need. As Davy pulled from the kiss, Gavin clamped his teeth, verging on painful, on Davy's bottom lip. One of his rare growls escaped. He saw light behind his eyes as he grabbed Gavin's wrists and pinned them above his head.

Davy had never felt such a strong need to dominate, to care for another person. He wanted to take away whatever pain Gavin was feeling. He made his way down Gavin's body, stopping to bite and lick along the way. He drew hickeys to the surface on Gavin's chest, unable to stop himself.

"So fucking sexy, Davy," Gavin said breathlessly.

Davy finally made it to his prize, taking Gavin's cock deep into his mouth. He gave no quarter as he sucked and stroked Gavin's balls and belly. Gavin started a brutal fucking of Davy's mouth, and Davy held on for every thrust.

"So good, Davy."

Gavin was like a man possessed. The head of his cock popped in and out of Davy's throat to the point his throat was almost raw. Davy's cock was so hard, and he was turned on so much by his ability to make Gavin let loose and feel things so deeply. Gavin was grunting and moaning shamelessly as the salty flavor of his precum flowed over Davy's tongue, lubing his throat along with the spit to make for one amazing taste. Davy was as lost in the act as Gavin.

But when Davy had said he intended to take care of Gavin, he meant it. He grabbed Gavin's thighs with both hands and pulled them apart, lifting them. He pulled off Gavin's cock and dove into the cleft of Gavin's ass, tasting the salty-sweetness of his hole. Davy had yet to find a part of Gavin's body that didn't taste fucking amazing.

Davy moaned into Gavin's ass as Gavin's hole yielded to the onslaught of his rimming. Davy employed the use of his finger, then two fingers, rough and hard. Gavin let out the most guttural moan Davy had ever heard him make.

"Fuck, yes. Fuck me hard, Davy. Just like that." Gavin forced his ass onto the finger-fucking with a fierceness that surprised Davy. Davy did as he was asked, though. He continued licking around his fingers to lube the way, then built a hard, brutal speed, crooking his fingers before every outward motion.

By the time Davy took Gavin back into his mouth, Gavin's body was limp, and he was babbling obscenities. Davy sucked hard, cheeks caving in with every upward pull of his mouth on Gavin's girth. He wanted to give him this. Gavin needed him, and that was all that mattered to Davy right now. The look Gavin gave him as Davy took care of his needs made Davy feel indestructible and like the most important person in the world.

"Davy. Fuck, I'm gonna come, babe." Davy stilled his fingers and crooked them over and over, using his other hand to stroke Gavin's cock, and his mouth doing quick laps of each of Gavin's balls. They pulled up under Davy's tongue, and Davy felt the moment the tension snapped, a split second before Gavin fucking *roared* with his release. "Oh, fuck. Fuck fuck, fuck, Davy. Babe. Jesus Christ!"

Davy forced Gavin's cock back into his gullet, eliciting another shout from Gavin as he shot himself into Davy, who kept a massage going with his fingers inside Gavin's ass. Gavin unloaded everything he had, giving Davy a piece of himself that no one else had. *Mine.* Davy didn't realize how turned-on he was just by the taste of Gavin and his name on Gavin's lips until he lowered his hips to the bed, and with just one rub against the sheets Davy's cock was shooting off. Davy sucked brutally on Gavin and moaned as he gave all he had to the point his balls ached.

"Goddamn, Davy!" Gavin grabbed Davy under the arms, pulled him up so they were face-to-face, and pilfered Davy's mouth with his tongue. They made out hot and heavy until Davy eased his fingers out of Gavin's ass, slowly, and then their kiss turned less demanding and more into a slow, loving, welcoming home. Gavin wrapped his arms and legs around Davy and held him tight, and Davy could swear the man was fighting tears. Davy's chest hurt, his heart bleeding for Gavin.

Gavin eased out of the kiss and placed his forehead against Davy's. "Thank you. Thank you, thank you, thank you," Gavin whispered brokenly. He opened eyes that were just a bit too bright for Davy's heart to handle. "I love you, Davy."

Davy choked on everything he wanted to say for fear he might make a fool of himself and cry *for* Gavin, if Gavin wouldn't cry for himself. He felt considerably less tense underneath Davy, though.

"I love you," Gavin said and kissed Davy's cheek and pulled him into a hug. When had they gotten here? When had Gavin snuck in so far that Davy couldn't imagine this man ever being anywhere but right here? Here in their bubble.

"Shh." Davy rubbed Gavin's hair, feeling him start to fall apart, the telltale wetness on Davy's chest and Gavin's quaking shoulders being all the clues Davy needed. "I love you too, Gav. I'm here." Davy held Gavin tighter and waited until Gavin cried himself out and drifted into a restless sleep.

DAVY TRUDGED up to his apartment. He'd had a long day. Actually he'd had a string of those days where he couldn't keep things refilled long enough to keep up with the demand of the crush of customers in his line. He'd had to call in someone to help by the time the noon rush hit, and he'd had to stay on until close because the lines had never stopped.

The day had been sunny and beautiful, the market full of tourists, the water-view park standing room only. The tip jar had overflowed, so the employee he'd had to call in was well compensated for coming in early. He was thankful he'd had the help. Now he just wanted to crawl into his bed and die until morning. The next day was his day off, but if the last few days were an indicator of what was to come, he imagined he'd be called in tomorrow as well. He almost whimpered at the thought of another ten hours on his feet.

Why had he taken the job as GM, anyway?

Oh yeah. It was a salaried position. With benefits. With his mom's survivor benefits, that meant he was much better off than other twenty-two-year-olds he knew. And in Seattle, that money was the difference between a decent apartment in town or a shitty room-share in SeaTac.

He shuddered at the thought of a roommate, especially a stranger. Although, in the last two weeks since Gavin's mom had shown up and turned everything on its ear, Gavin had been crashing with Davy on his daybed, which grew more and more uncomfortable with two people having to share it. He was beginning to think he should have splurged on a bed. He had never expected anyone else to share his space with him, though, so he hadn't planned accordingly.

When he opened the door to his apartment, the first thing he noticed was the smell of garlic. He sniffed the air appreciatively.

"Ohmigod, did you order Italian?" Davy asked, unable to keep the longing from his voice. He'd not had a chance to even eat lunch today.

Gavin laughed and came around from the kitchen area, then gave Davy a quick kiss. When he pulled back, he looked Davy over and frowned. "You look wiped."

"Ugh. I am. Another day with no break."

"Davy…," Gavin scolded. Davy couldn't help but smile. It had been a long time since he'd come home to be mothered. And Gavin was good at it. "You're not supposed to smile when I'm fussing at you."

Davy laughed. "It's just that you sounded like my mother."

"Awesome," Gavin said drily. Davy placed a kiss on his thinned lips before wandering in to drop his book bag and keys in the corner. He rolled his shoulders, enjoying not having the weight on them. Gavin walked up behind him and kissed the nape of his neck.

"You gotta stop working so much, babe," Gavin said.

"Says the trust-fund kid."

Gavin punched Davy playfully. Davy knew he hadn't dipped into the trust fund for anything other than school books or his vehicle, otherwise it still sat in the bank where he'd put a restriction on it so he couldn't touch it 'til he was twenty-five. Davy was surprised at some of Gavin's responsible decisions. They seemed so at odds with what people assumed of Gavin.

135

Davy plopped down on the daybed where Gavin had his homework spread out and stacked it neatly before sliding it next to his feet beneath the coffee table. Gavin wandered over with two beers and two plates piled high with chicken Alfredo from their favorite Italian eatery that delivered to Davy's building.

"Beer and pasta. The two basic food groups," Gavin said as Davy took a plate for himself. Gavin set his plate on the table and popped the top off a beer, then offered it to Davy. Davy took it, receiving another peck on the lips from Gavin. He found himself amazed at how affectionate Gavin could be. Especially since the intense night after Gavin's mom had shown up and thrown Gavin into a tailspin. Gavin had truly opened up to Davy. Davy was okay being Gavin's life raft right now. It was nice being needed. It had also been beautiful watching the change in Gavin as he got to know his little brother. Ollie and Gavin were so much alike it was freaky, and it often made Ray choke with emotion. Davy caught the old guy getting weepy a couple times and had sworn his secrecy.

"Oh, before I forget…," Davy said. He took a long pull from his beer, then set it and his plate on the table and started rooting through his pockets. "Ah, here it is." He pulled a key out and held it out to Gavin.

Gavin stared at it for a moment. "What's that?"

Davy looked at the key, wondering if he'd hallucinated and pulled out a paper clip instead. He was exhausted enough he could imagine having done just that. But when he looked he saw that he did, in fact, hold a key. "Well, it looks like a key."

"To what?"

Davy felt lost. "Um, my apartment?" Or was it? He wasn't sure of much, and Gavin didn't look much surer than Davy felt.

"Yeah, but why?"

"Well, Gavin, I figured you're tired of having to wait at the shop for me to get off so you can come home, and I know you have to get sick of sitting around here all day on those that you don't have class. This way you can come and go."

Gavin looked at Davy then at the key. Davy was tired of this game and very hungry, so he took Gavin's hand that wasn't holding his beer, placed the key in his palm, and closed the fingers around it. Gavin opened his fingers and stared at the key. Davy sighed and turned to pick up his plate.

"That's it?"

"What?" Davy said, exasperation at Gavin's weirdness bleeding into his tone.

"It's just for necessity? So I don't have to wait on you?" Gavin asked, still looking at the key.

Davy sat, eyebrow quirked, wondering what the hell was wrong for a second until everything fell into place and he felt the proverbial lightbulb go on. "Oh!" Davy laughed.

Gavin turned and looked at him quizzically.

"Shut up, Gav. You know I want you to have a key. It's exactly what it means. I just figured you already knew that since I let you stay here alone all the time. Geez."

"So, you're not just giving me a key. You're *giving* me a key?"

"Geez, you weirdo." Davy smiled fondly at Gavin, who was looking uncertainly at the key again. "Of course I am." He leaned in and kissed Gavin on the cheek. When Gavin didn't say anything, Davy wondered if, as usual, he'd misread Gavin's signs. God, he wished he knew how social situations worked. He'd never given a guy his key. He didn't know how the hell this worked and he was guessing he'd fucked it up. He looked at his plate and poked his fork around, suddenly losing his appetite to embarrassment. "That is, if you want it. You could always just give it back when you're not staying here so much." Davy said it quietly.

Davy didn't know how, but suddenly he found himself flat on his back, Gavin in his face kissing his cheeks, lips, nose…. "What the—"

Gavin kept on with his ridiculous kissing until Davy squirmed his way from underneath him, laughing. "What the hell?" he asked he asked, taken… well, taken aback. Literally.

Gavin looked at him with a childlike smile, then held up the key. "You *gave* me your key!"

"Uh. Yeah?" Davy was just fucking with him now. He was excited that Gavin had wanted it to be a *key*. If he hadn't been so damn tired lately, he'd have put on more of a show of giving the key, but he'd thought to stop after work today and didn't want to forget the damn thing in his pocket.

Davy laughed as Gavin rolled him down onto the floor and kissed him, wet and sloppy.

Gavin pulled back, still smiling wide. "You're fucking awesome, Davy Cooper."

Davy blushed, but his cheeks hurt from smiling so much.

"Up. Up. Get up and eat," Gavin said as he helped Davy up. "I've got dirty things to do to you."

Davy knew Gavin probably heard him swallow. He wanted to ask if they could just skip dinner, but his stomach loudly protested that idea before he could even form the question.

They made quick work of eating. Davy didn't even have to rush himself. As hungry as he was, he practically inhaled his food. When he finished his food and a second beer, he was afraid sex would be out of the question, though, as his tired muscles started dragging.

Gavin took his dishes from him. "You go shower. You look so tired it's making my muscles ache too."

"Sympathy aches?" Davy teased, but his humor was halfhearted at best. He was bone-weary.

"Go. Shower." Gavin used a plate to point to the bathroom.

Davy huffed. "Yes, Mother."

Gavin kicked Davy in the ass as Davy walked away.

WHEN DAVY stepped into the shower, he sighed as the warm water sluiced over his skin, carrying away the sweat and grime of his seemingly endless day. The more the spray relaxed his muscles, the more his body sagged. He had to put a hand against the tiled wall to hold himself up as his body lost its will to carry on.

He shook himself to perk up long enough to shampoo his hair and lather himself with body wash. He hadn't even finished rinsing when he had to hold his arm out again to steady himself. He couldn't believe how fast sleep was attempting to claim him. He let his eyes drift shut for just a moment.

He wasn't sure what woke him, but he knew he hadn't slept long because he was still standing and the water was still hot. Chilly air breezed over his legs, then strong arms wrapped around his middle.

"Poor, sleepy Davy." Gavin's voice tickled his senses. Gavin pulled Davy back against his chest, where Davy fell back and drifted for a minute, loving the relaxing comfort of Gavin's hands gently rubbing up and down his front and the gentle kisses on his neck. Davy's cock responded to the gentle ministrations and to the long, hard cock riding the crack of his ass. Gavin chuckled in his ear. Davy sucked in a breath when Gavin cupped his balls and squeezed. Fuck, that felt so good. Gavin gave Davy's cock a few tugs, then stopped, leaving Davy bereft as his cock jumped, as if searching for Gavin's touch.

Davy opened his eyes to see Gavin turn off the water. "Hold yourself up, babe," Gavin said. Davy cringed when the shower curtain opened, letting in the cold air. His flesh crawled with goose bumps. Davy must have been out of it, because he hadn't noticed Gavin leave the shower and was suddenly wrapping a towel around him and helping him dry off. Davy felt so cared for. He still couldn't reconcile this Gavin with the one he'd met what felt like so long ago. Although, the better he'd gotten to know Gavin, the more he'd realized that other shit was posturing and self-preservation.

This Gavin was the real Gavin, and he was loving and considerate. And he got excited over getting a key to Davy's apartment and helped Davy dry off when he was too tired to do it himself.

Davy looked at Gavin and leaned in for a kiss. Gavin's kiss was not one of his usual steamy, turned-on kisses, instead a kiss that said welcome home. *Home.* Davy found more and more that being with Gavin was the most he'd felt like being home since his mother had been alive.

Gavin took Davy by both hands and led him to the daybed, where he pulled Davy close. Davy looked into his eyes and saw all that love just shining in there and was almost overwhelmed with it. Gavin held him up with one arm around his waist, then put his other hand between them and tugged Davy's cock leisurely. Gavin kissed his neck, his chest, and nibbled a nipple. Davy's head fell back as he succumbed to his release that crested like a gentle wave carrying him back to land.

The next time Davy opened his eyes, they were lying down, sheet pulled over their naked bodies. Gavin had pulled Davy so his back was flush to his chest and wrapped his arm around Davy's waist. Davy sighed contentedly.

"I love you so much, Davy."

"I love you, Gavin." Davy lay quietly for a moment, then whispered, "I'm glad you were happy about the key."

Gavin hooked a leg between Davy's. "Best gift I've ever gotten."

Davy rolled his eyes. He was strangely wide-awake now that he was all tucked in with Gavin. He'd been meaning to ask for days, but they hadn't had a chance, so he finally brought up the elephant in the room, knowing Gavin was much more agreeable post-orgasm. "How's it going with your family?"

Gavin grunted.

"That good, huh?"

Gavin was silent for another moment. "Shit, Davy, what do you want me to say?"

Davy patted Gavin's hand. "Nothing. I just was asking, okay?"

Gavin was quiet for another minute. "Yeah. I'm sorry. It's just…. Stressful."

"You know I'm here if you wanna talk, right?"

Gavin hugged tighter to Davy as if he were trying to crawl inside him. "I know. I'm just all mixed up right now. You're the only thing right in my life right now. I kinda like keeping the rest of it out of here. I don't want it in the middle of us."

"I understand. Whatever you need," Davy said. And he meant it. Whatever Gavin needed he could do. He could be strong for Gavin. He could talk to strangers or… babysit children for Gavin. "Can I just say one thing?"

"Sure."

Davy inhaled, nervous as to how Gavin might react to what he was about to say. He'd been practicing it in his head for days and hoped it came out right. "I know what happened with your mom in the past was fucked-up. And I know you can't just make that go away, and nothing my mom did was that bad, but there's this anger I have toward my mom that I'll never get to forgive her for. She died. She never even knew I *was* angry. And it hurts. It eats you up inside some days. So if she's trying—I'm not saying you have to forgive her now, or ever—but maybe you should at least talk to her about it. Scream at her. Get it out."

Gavin had stopped breathing at some point as Davy tumbled over his words. Davy closed his eyes tight, hoping he hadn't pissed Gavin off. "I know it's none of my business—"

Gavin put a hand over Davy's mouth. "Of course it's your business. You're looking out for me. I get that."

Davy thought maybe Gavin had something else to say, but not long after that, Gavin was snoring. He wasn't sleeping peacefully, clinging to Davy, but he was obviously done with the subject.

Davy hoped he hadn't said something stupid. He really did just want Gavin to be okay, and Gavin didn't seem as though he was dealing with this.

Davy wrapped both his arms around the arm Gavin had thrown around his chest and hugged it. His last thought before falling asleep was of how much he just wanted Gavin to be happy.

CHAPTER EIGHTEEN

GAVIN HELPED Oliver put the final sticker on the plastic model Chevelle he'd bought for them to work on together. He'd taken Oliver to his favorite model store in the market and let Oliver pick out one of the kiddy models the kid was probably still too young to do, but Gavin had done most of it while Oliver chatted away in his lap. Gavin loved it because building models had always been his way of clearing his head. He'd done a couple hundred in his life and sharing it with his little brother was cool. He'd never shared this with anyone.

"All right, little dude. We're all done," Gavin announced.

"All done?" Oliver asked excitedly and tried to reach for it.

Gavin stopped his pudgy little arm and laughed at Oliver's enthusiasm. "Whoa, man. We gotta let it dry first. But yeah. It's all done."

"Cooool!" Oliver yelled it louder than necessary, but Oliver did everything louder than necessary. Which Gavin found strange, since Oliver seemed weirdly respectful and careful with everything else. From his manners to his handling of breakable objects, the boy was eerily reticent. But his voice.... Loud. This kid was fucking loud.

Oliver bounced in Gavin's lap. "I go tell Grampa!"

I'm sure he heard. Gavin chuckled and helped Oliver down out of his lap. "Just remember not to jump in his lap, little guy."

142

"I not little guy!" Oliver hollered. "I big boy!"

Gavin held his hands up in apology. "My bad. You're so right. You are. Well, be a big guy and go tell Grampa, quietly, and don't jump in his lap."

Oliver patted Gavin's knee. "I know. Grampa is sick and that makes you sad."

"Yeah." Gavin was amazed at the things the kid picked up on.

"It okay, Gavvy. I love you." Oliver smiled, threw a hug around Gavin's middle, then ran off to the den to find Ray.

Gavin sucked in a breath and held it. Who knew the kid could make him so damn weepy? *I knew I was screwed.*

As Gavin dumped leftover plastic into the recycle bins underneath the counter, Carmen came in through the swinging door. She paused for a moment when she saw him. She'd been politely staying out of his space unless he came to her or she had a question about the household.

"Hi," he said.

"Hi, Gavin," Carmen replied with a hopeful smile.

Another reason Gavin had enjoyed working on the model car with Oliver was that it had given him time to reflect on what Davy had said a week ago about his own mother dying before he'd been able to forgive her. He'd needed to really consider what he might say to her.

He figured simple was best. If she wanted to try, he'd meet her on the road. Not halfway, but he'd take a step toward her.

"I told Oliver that Sean and I would take him to see the guys throw the fish down at the market. They were done for the day when I took him to the model store. Would you wanna come?"

He could tell she had to contain herself from jumping at the offer. "Only if you don't mind," she said, keeping her tone even.

He chewed the inside of his cheek for a second, then made up his mind. "Yeah. Yeah, it'd be cool if you came."

She pulled her lips between her teeth, probably trying to hold back a smile. "Will Davy be coming?"

143

Gavin curled up his lip. "No, but we'll probably swing by Bart's to get Oliver some ice cream. If it's a problem—"

"No, no that's not what I was saying, Gavin. I just wondered," she said earnestly. He couldn't tell if she was backtracking or if she'd really not meant anything by it. He was convinced she didn't like that he was with Davy, and he couldn't imagine why. Or maybe she was just jealous, as usual, that his life wasn't as shitty as hers had been at his age. Fuck if he cared.

"Well, we thought we'd go tomorrow since Sean is off, so we'll probably swing by to get you guys around noon."

"Oh. You're staying at Davy's again?"

"Well, you're in my room."

"There are guest rooms."

"And you're pushing it."

She shut her mouth against whatever she was about to say. She looked as though she was thinking over the best way to say whatever she had in mind. "It'd be nice to have you home for dinner one night. I thought I'd cook something."

Gavin frowned thoughtfully. "Since when do you cook, Carmen?"

"I wish you wouldn't call me that."

Gavin crossed his arms over his chest and looked at her hard.

She shrank under his gaze. "Well, would you and Davy have dinner here tomorrow night, then?"

Gavin stewed it over for a minute. Tomorrow was supposed to be Davy's half day at work, so he didn't imagine Davy would have a problem coming for dinner. "Sure. It'd do Ray good to see the whole family here."

Carmen put on her fake smile at his using the word family, and he resisted the urge to pounce.

"It's a date," she said.

"Cool. Well, I'm gonna go say good night to Ray and Oliver. I've got homework to do."

"See you in the morning," she said. He gathered his box of model-building materials. Carmen stopped him with a light touch to his arm as he walked by her toward the door. She pulled her hand back quickly, but he still stopped. "I appreciate you asking me to come. And for agreeing to dinner."

He searched her face for a moment. "Cool" was all he could think to say. "See you tomorrow."

Gotta start somewhere.

AS GAVIN drove everyone home, Oliver passed out in his car seat that was buckled in the backseat of the truck. Gavin thought their day out hadn't been as awkward as he'd feared it might be. Oliver had been mesmerized by the massive flying fish as the men at the market tossed them back and forth, putting on one of Seattle's most well-known tourist attractions. He'd been thrilled about the loud way Oliver got thrilled over everything when he received a high five from one of the fishmongers for dropping the tip money Davy had sent with them into the jar. Gavin had to hand it to Davy. For someone who was horrified he didn't know what the hell to do with a kid, Davy knew what would make Oliver's day. And getting a high five from one of the "magic fish guys" had been a highlight Oliver had babbled about over and over.

One thing that hadn't surprised Gavin was how well Carmen and Sean had gotten along. He knew Sean would keep the peace for Gavin and Oliver's sake, and Carmen still had the old charm that, if you didn't know what ugliness she's once used it for, could completely beguile you.

When they made it back to the house, Sean took his leave, claiming tiredness, but Gavin suspected he'd been worn out keeping up the nice front with Carmen. Sean may not have known about what happened with Max, but he'd met Gavin at his lowest and been around to see the repercussions of Gavin's bad teenage years. He didn't seem quite ready to be civil to her for long increments of time.

Gavin understood, but he was still on a high from spending the day with one of his best friends and his little brother. He was still totally shocked at the idea of having a little brother—you didn't get used to that overnight—but after a few weeks the weirdness was wearing off, and he fell in love with the kid (and his loud-ass mouth) a little more every day, though getting him to say it enthusiastically just now would take pulling teeth. He still had a rep to protect.

When he'd said the latter out loud to Davy in the privacy of Davy's apartment, he'd been openly mocked. Damn that guy for knowing him too well. And wasn't that a whole other overwhelming development? Gavin wasn't sure where all of the insanity of domestic bliss had come from over the past few months, but it was so different that he barely recognized it. He was thankful every morning he woke up in Davy's arms that he'd found Davy before Gavin's mother and Oliver had appeared in his den, or he may have lost the chance to enjoy his brother, and maybe—maybe—give his mom a chance.

A few times throughout the day, he'd noticed how Carmen looked at his interactions with Oliver, affection and hope open on her face. She seemed so bright, and her eyes were clearer than he'd seen in such a long time before he'd moved to Seattle. He still had too much baggage to just up and give a shit that she was apparently sober for real this time, but he felt the stupid tingles of hope in there somewhere.

He kept Davy's words in his head. No matter what horrible mistakes she'd made, she was his mother. He'd regret it more on his side for not trying. And more than anything, this was for Oliver. He needed to make sure that even if his mom fell off the wagon again, Oliver always knew he'd have Gavin around.

He told himself this was all for Oliver. The small child in his heart who called out for his mother's love all those years begged to differ, though. Damn that inner child.

When they got home, Oliver woke and went from sleepy to a very loud babbling ball of energy in short order. Davy was already there helping Ray with a Sudoku when Gavin and the others wandered into the house. Gavin's shoulders slumped in relief when Davy and his grandfather looked up at him with welcoming smiles.

"Davy, good to see you," Carmen said cheerfully. If anyone else questioned the sincerity in her voice, they kept it to themselves, though she had seemed to warm to him more after her first visit. Maybe she just needed to get used to him. Davy's quiet demeanor and eyes that seemed able to read you like a book could be unnerving if you didn't know how genuinely kind the guy was. To someone like Carmen, who'd probably dealt with few genuine people in her life, Davy's frequent appraisal of her in social situations was probably intimidating, especially knowing how much Gavin cared for him.

"Hi, guys," Davy said, standing from where he'd been sitting in a kitchen chair he'd brought out so he could be next to Ray.

Gavin met Davy halfway and they shared a chaste kiss on the lips. Gavin didn't realize how much he'd needed that to steady him, but he felt better.

"Did you have fun seeing the fish, Ollie?" And the question of whether everything had gone okay settled in the space between Davy and Gavin. Gavin gave Davy the hint of a smile and nodded for reassurance.

Oliver took an audible inhalation that Gavin had learned meant his brother was about to burst with information, but before Oliver opened his mouth, Carmen put her hand over it, laughing. "Use your inside voice," she warned playfully.

Everyone laughed at Oliver's eye roll. He must have gotten that from Davy, because whether Davy knew it or not, he rolled his eyes at Gavin a lot.

And he was off. Oliver started telling Davy and Ray about the fish and getting a high five and feeding seagulls in the park (which was frowned upon). Ray and Davy oohed and ahhed in all the right places to satisfy Oliver. At some point Carmen excused herself to cook dinner.

For a while there was a flurry of activity thanks to the two-and-half-foot-tall tornado known affectionately as Oliver. There was showing off things they'd purchased in the comic book store where Sean worked, Oliver's input on the Sudoku puzzle (no one destroys that hard work like a three-year-old), and the constant begging for the ice

147

cream Davy had accidentally mentioned that he'd brought from work for dessert. They must have heard "just one bite" twelve times if they heard it once.

"You're being a brat. Go see if Mommy needs any help with dinner," Gavin instructed.

"Okay!" Oliver hollered in Davy's face, making Davy rear back and Ray, who was sitting next to them, wince. As soon as Oliver was through the kitchen door, the silence that followed was almost deafening and the three men looked at each other slowly.

Then they burst with laughter.

God, Gavin felt so light, even more so when Davy moved into his arms and hugged him, bussing Gavin's cheek. "So it really went well?"

"Yeah, yeah it did," Gavin said honestly. "It was a good day."

"That's my boy," Ray said merrily.

He knew Ray was thrilled that things were working out even if progress was slow. Gavin was glad Ray got to meet Oliver and, yes, that he'd gotten to see the prodigal daughter once more before—

Gavin couldn't even think it. The day was going too damn well. With Davy in his arms and Ray having such a good day, his mind rebelled against any negativity, even where Carmen was concerned. He folded into Davy and enjoyed the silent happiness of the moment. Until Oliver barreled through the swinging door hollering, "Dinner's ready!" Gavin and Davy shared an exasperated look.

"Wasn't it you that said that kid was cute?" Gavin asked.

Davy shook his head and pointing, said, "Hell no. Not me. I'm pretty sure it was you."

Yeah, it was Gavin. So he had a soft spot for the loud little fucker. What could he say?

"Well somebody's gotta make up for the talking you don't do," Ray fussed. Davy's face flushed, and Gavin had to put his hand over his mouth to cover his grin as Ray stood from his chair and headed toward the dining room, mumbling, "Quietest boy I've ever met in my life."

Davy talked so much to Gavin that Gavin had forgotten just how quiet Davy could be around other people sometimes. He knew for a fact Davy hadn't really had any one-on-one time with Carmen, but Carmen and Davy both seemed to dance around any situation that would call for that. Not that Gavin could blame Davy in the least.

Gavin kissed Davy on his nose, then took his hand, following Ray into the dining room. Carmen and Oliver were setting the table. Well, Carmen was setting the table and Oliver was playing with the silverware, but she thanked him for the help all the same. Gavin and Davy took a seat across from Carmen and Oliver, Ray at the head of the table.

Gavin looked at the spread in surprise. Carmen had never been much of a cook when he was growing up. That was why he had developed some decent skills in the kitchen. He'd spent hours watching the Food Network, perfecting a few random dishes. (He still watched it, if he was honest.) Carmen had prepared a decent dinner, though. Roast beef, potatoes, and some mixed veggies.

The table was silent as everyone passed dishes around, serving themselves. Gavin was impressed when he took his first bite and the roast actually melted in his mouth. He'd expected it to suck.

"This is real good, Carmen," Ray said. You could hear the shock in his voice. Carmen beamed with pride.

"Yeah, Carmen. Did you take a cooking class or something?" Gavin asked. Carmen's face dimmed. Gavin didn't mean to insult. He was genuinely curious. "No, no. It's really good. I just don't remember you cooking much."

Carmen picked around her food for a moment before answering. "I picked up some stuff on this last trip to rehab."

"Hmm" was Gavin's only response. He had to give her kudos for honesty.

Silence descended on the table again for a few minutes. All that could be heard was Oliver's humming to himself and the clinking of silverware on plates. Carmen cleared her throat, making Gavin turn his attention to her. "So, Davy, you're so quiet. Do you like it?"

149

Gavin looked from Carmen to Davy, who looked unsure as to what to say. Ah, good ol' predictable Davy, squirming now that all the attention was on him. Gavin reached under the table and placed his hand on Davy's knee for comfort. Davy swallowed the bite he'd just taken and licked his lips. Oh shit. That tongue made wicked thoughts dance through Gavin's mind. *Wrong time, wrong place.*

Davy looked knowingly at Gavin before answering Carmen. "Uh, yeah. It's great. Thanks so much for having me tonight."

Polite and to the point. Gavin knew that wouldn't be enough for Carmen, though.

"So are you in school?"

Davy looked at Gavin again then answered, "Yes, ma'am. I do correspondence through U-Dub."

"Any particular major?"

"Well, I'm taking mostly business courses."

Carmen's face held that smile that could have been either genuine or annoyed, which was the usual way she looked at Davy. "That's nice," she said, and Gavin thought maybe she'd leave Davy alone. "So how did you and Gavin meet?" No such luck.

"Carmen," Ray and Gavin said at the same time.

"What?" Her face was all wide-eyed innocence.

"Ha! You said that at the same time. Silly." Everyone laughed at Oliver's outburst.

Carmen turned her attention back to Davy. "Sorry. I just want to get to know you. You obviously mean a great deal to Gavin and Daddy."

Gavin frowned, wondering when she'd taken to calling Ray Daddy. He'd always known her to call him Ray with the highest amount of distaste.

"Oh, it's okay," Davy assured. "Um, he came in to my work." Davy looked at Gavin from the corner of his eye, grinning. "A lot."

Ray snorted and got a "Bless you, Grampa," from Oliver.

"He'd come by once or twice a week with his whole group of friends. He'd hang back and leave me his number."

Carmen looked amused.

"He's a persistent little shit, isn't he?" Ray snorted.

"Hey, hey. I just go after what I want," Gavin corrected, sniffing delicately. "Besides"—he squeezed Davy's knee and stared at his profile for a moment—"it worked, didn't it?"

Davy turned to Gavin with a smile, the one Gavin knew was just for him, and placed his hand on top of Gavin's.

"Oh, you two are sickening."

Gavin snapped his head to Carmen, ready to pounce on her. He'd just known she had a problem with it, and her words sent a bolt of hot anger right through him. But when he looked at her, she was looking at them with a teasing smile. Davy nudged Gavin's shoulder, obviously having picked up on what Gavin's initial thought had been. Gavin felt himself blush, and didn't that beat all? He felt like an ass.

"Well, I think you two are cute together," Carmen said, shocking the hell out of Gavin again.

He looked at her slack-jawed until Davy laughed at him. After shooting a glare at Davy, Gavin decided to move the conversation off them. "So, Carmen, what are your plans? When do you have to go back to Maine?"

"Well." Carmen looked to Ray, who nodded for her to continue. "Well, I finished beauty school finally. I thought I'd apply for my license out here. I'd like to bring Oliver here—home—for good, if you'd be okay with that."

Gavin blinked. He could tell how pleased Ray was by this turn of events, and if he was honest, the idea of having Oliver around for good was awesome. He'd been dreading finally getting to know his little brother only to lose him, because no way was Gavin going back to Maine. There were entirely too many bad memories to drown him there. He wasn't sure how he felt about having *her* around permanently, though. Things had been going well, but he was way too mixed up inside for the final vote to come from him.

"If that's what you want, it'd be great having Ollie around," Gavin hedged. Damn Davy and that nickname. It had just slipped out, but it was enough to let Carmen know Gavin was not as indifferent as his posturing may suggest.

"That's settled, then," Ray said grandly. Everyone looked at him. "What? Can't I just pretend I run this family for five minutes?"

"Yeah, good luck with that, Daddy." Carmen kissed Ray on the cheek as she cleared her plate and rose. She took Oliver's and Ray's with her to the kitchen. Ray harrumphed in offense. Carmen stuck her head out the kitchen door. "If you boys will go to the den, I'll bring out the ice cream Davy brought."

Gavin and Ray rose. Davy helped Oliver out of his booster seat and told him to go play with his new cars while Mommy got ice cream. They all watched as Oliver darted off to the living room screaming, "Ice cream!" Well, they could at least be grateful he'd been quiet enough for them to have a conversation over dinner.

"I'm gonna help clear the table," Davy said.

"You sure?" Gavin asked.

"Positive. You guys go chill. You've been running around all day, and she's right. I haven't been alone with her. If she's gonna be around for a while, then we should get used to being around each other."

"Okay. Yell if you need backup."

Davy just rolled his eyes and started picking up dishes from the table.

Gavin walked into the den where Ray had Oliver in his lap. As excited as Oliver had been for ice cream, apparently the long day had caught up with him in the five minutes since he'd left the table, because his eyes were shuttering as Ray read something from a crime novel to him. Probably not the most appropriate bedtime story for a kid, but it was Ray, after all. Gavin watched contentedly from the couch as Oliver lost his fight to stay awake.

TROUBLE & THE WALLFLOWER

"You're really happy, huh?" Gavin asked Ray. The serenity in Ray's eyes when he said "Very happy" was all Gavin could ask for the old guy right now. Ever since Ray had announced to Gavin that the prognosis for his pancreatic cancer was bad, that he had less than a year to go and the radiation had failed, Ray's eyes had been haunted. Ray worried for Gavin, grieved for his daughter. Now their family was together—still broken but working to mend—and that gave Ray peace.

Gavin could live with that. And he'd remember that look on Ray's face forever.

lll the

CHAPTER NINETEEN

DAVY SAT in front of Ray's house. He'd been there, pacing for twenty minutes before he sat down on the bench on the porch. He wasn't sure what he was going to say, but he had to do something. He was so angry. Furious. He'd never known anger in his life like he felt then.

Just the day before everything had seemed so hopeful. Gavin had seemed happy when his mother announced over dinner that she and Oliver might be staying in Washington. Davy was convinced that decision was for the best when he and Carmen had come in with dessert to find Ray and Oliver sleeping together in Ray's easy chair and Gavin looking so happy that Davy's stomach fluttered.

That made it all the harder to get his thoughts together. *My, what a difference twenty-four hours could make.* Part of him said he should have talked to Gavin, but a deeper need to protect had driven him to acting before he really thought all of this through. He'd gotten on the bus and called his Uncle Drew and ranted about the conversation he'd had with Sean just hours earlier. Drew agreed that Carmen needed to be confronted.

Drew had been so supportive of Davy and Gavin's relationship, even when he'd learned of Gavin's reputation. He'd just said that everyone has a past. Davy figured it was because he was still shocked that he actually had a boyfriend. So Davy had assumed Drew would say to run fast and far when he called to say Gavin was probably going to have a meltdown when

154

he found out his mother was off the wagon she may have never been on. But Drew had said he knew Davy could handle it.

"You're stronger than you give yourself credit for. I know I've treated you with kid gloves, but you care about him, right?"

"I love him," Davy said fiercely.

Drew chuckled into the phone. "Go stand up for your man. Go stand up for your new family, Davy. You may not get another chance to have one."

Davy could hear the regret, the sadness in Drew's voice. His uncle's words were exactly what he needed. He just didn't know what to say. He thought back over the information he had and thought how best to handle Carmen.

Sean had come into the shop as Davy was getting ready to leave work. "I need to talk," he announced. Davy had never known Sean to look so flustered. He was usually pretty well put together.

"Okay." Davy frowned, waved to the girl who was taking over the counter for the afternoon shift, and followed Sean to a booth.

"Yesterday, when I was with Gavin and his mom, I noticed something," Sean said, fiddling with his hands, obviously uncomfortable.

"What?"

"Gavin's mom went to the bathroom and was taking a while, so I hung back to wait on her while Gavin went on to the comic book store with Oliver...."

Davy waited until he thought Sean might not finish his thought. Davy gestured impatiently, worried now. "And...?"

"I got tired of waiting, so I went toward the bathrooms to see if maybe she was talking on her phone or something."

"What was she doing?" Davy wasn't sure he wanted to know if the strife on Sean's face meant anything.

"She was in one of the downstairs bars, drinking." Sean's voice was so sad.

"I guess she wasn't drinking juice, huh?" Davy asked, lamely.

"Try a double vodka, neat."

155

"Shit," Davy hissed. His blood boiled.

"I can't figure out what to say to Gavin. I just knew I couldn't do it in front of the kid and I sure as hell couldn't do it when all of you were having a big family night last night. I didn't know what to do." Sean was clearly beating himself up.

Davy put his hand on Sean's, knowing better than anyone how it felt not to know what the hell to do when it came to others and their feelings. "Hey, don't worry. I'll do something, okay?"

Sean looked at Davy dubiously. Davy knew his social ineptitude and less than aggressive attitude didn't inspire much confidence, but this was Gavin and Ray and Oliver. Davy thought of all those times he'd seen Gavin look at him with trust in his eyes, making Davy constantly feel as though he was a hero.

"I'll handle this," Davy said.

Sean must have seen something he liked in Davy's eyes, because he smiled sadly and patted Davy's hand on the table. "Take care of our boy, okay? This is going to crush him."

"I know." And Davy did know. That was why it was imperative he find the right words to say to Carmen. He didn't know how alcoholism worked. He'd thought his mom's agoraphobia was difficult, but at least it hadn't made her a liar. Or a monster. Davy knew Gavin still struggled mostly because of what happened with Max, so his trust would be completely destroyed if he found out he'd let Carmen in a little for Oliver's and Ray's sake, only to be lied to again so she could go get drunk while on their first-ever family day.

Davy wanted to fucking puke, he was so angry.

Finally he stood and wiped his sweaty palms on his jeans. He thought he might talk to Ray first and hoped Carmen wasn't around right now. He eased in through the front door, not bothering to take off his shoes this time. He made his way from room to room, only to find no Ray. *Damn.* Davy looked at his watch. Ray must be napping. It was the time of the day that Ray was known to have a lie down after taking his afternoon meds.

Before turning to leave, Davy was stopped by quiet murmurings from the kitchen. He went for the door but realized the voice on the other side was Carmen. The conversation was one-sided, so Davy figured she must be on the phone. He was about to turn to leave, disgusted at the slight slurring of her words, until he caught her side of the conversation.

"…need the money."

Davy frowned.

"I know, but Ray needed convincing I was going to stick around after he died…. He wants someone watching over Gavin and that judgmental little shit he's dating."

Davy wondered why she thought he was judgmental. He knew some people said that was what they thought when they first met him. Silence was apparently intimidating. He hadn't been judgmental of Carmen, not once. He'd wanted it to work out for Gavin's sake.

Up until now. Now his blood was so hot in his veins he felt it might burn through his skin. Anger was *definitely* a new thing for Davy, and he wasn't sure he liked it, but the more he heard of her conversation, the more Hulk-like his anger made him.

"I don't fucking know. I'm just ready for the old guy to get it over with. Gavin doesn't need me. Never did. I'm really doing him a favor leaving."

"Yes. You are," Davy snarled as he shoved through the swinging door, unable to stop himself. "Are you fucking kidding me?" His heart hammered. It hurt. So bad. Physically and emotionally, he hurt from the anger and for Gavin.

Carmen jumped up from the chair she was sitting in, knocking over the Solo cup she had been drinking from and dropping the phone. The room smelled like a bar. "D-Davy. Get the fuck out!" She tried for righteous indignation, but he stalked to her, assaulted by the strong smell of vodka that hovered around her like a cloud. The point of vodka was to be a neutral spirit, hard to smell unless you were bathed in the stuff. How had they missed this?

"You must be really good at lying if you can cover this shit up." Davy picked up the cup she'd knocked over and sniffed. Straight vodka. "And no way you're drinking that much and still standing here if you've been sober for a while, so don't even give me that bullshit." Davy had had enough booze in his life to know how tolerance worked.

157

"I guess you're going to tell Gavin."

Carmen crossed her hands over her chest and jutted her chin out, looking so much like Gavin. Davy was so sad seeing his lover in this pathetic creature's face. He'd never felt such contempt.

"How could you do this to them? Gavin was trying so hard. And he loves Oliver so much. And Ray? How could you say that? He's dying!"

"You really are fucking naïve, aren't you?" Carmen mocked.

"Fuck you, lady."

"No, fuck you, *kid*. People aren't good. So you can stop looking like you expected better. That disappointed look stopped working on me a long fucking time ago."

Carmen's eyes looked lifeless. Davy guessed she was finally able to be real for once. "I'm sad for you, that you think that. My mom thought that too, and she never left her house."

"She was a smart lady, then."

"No!" Davy's anger boiled over. He clenched his fists at his sides. "My mom was wrong. You're wrong." Carmen's face was cynical, as if saying, *Oh, really?* "Yes. You're both wrong. I don't know what happened with Ray and you, that's not why I'm here. But Oliver. Oliver is good. And Gavin, he's good. And he's strong. Despite you and all the damage you did to him, Gavin's one of the good ones."

Carmen lost a bit of her fight. "Yeah. I don't know how, but he didn't turn out so bad, huh?"

"No thanks to you."

"Look, you judgmental—"

"Save it!" Davy felt every word rising from his heart of hearts, blazing with the need to protect his family. His family. Not hers. She'd lost the right to call them family with the first lie, and lost her right to be around them with the last one.

"You, Carmen, are going to pack your shit and get the fuck out of here. No money, no thanks—hell, I don't care if you fucking get no good-bye on your way out the door. Go back to Rockland or wherever it is you crawled out of and leave Gavin alone. You're done hurting him."

She looked at him with a mixture of disgust and begrudging respect. "Well, you got more balls than I thought, kid."

"More than you wanna know, lady."

"And I suppose if I don't go you'll just tell them anyways and they'll kick me out." It was a statement, not a question. She knew from the way Davy glared at her there was no way out of this. No one would trust her over Davy, and with good reason.

"Thank you," she whispered.

Davy reared back. "What?" Davy sounded shocked to his own ears.

She laughed derisively. "You just saved them from me. You know, I meant it when I said Gavin never needed me. He's better off without me."

Davy ran his fingers through his hair and said sadly, "You're wrong about one thing. Gavin did need you. He needed his mom. Like Oliver does. And for the love of all that's holy, get yourself together for that kid. I know I can't stop you from taking him, but don't let him lose Gavin. Let them keep in touch. Please."

She nodded silently. "You should go to him."

"What? Why?" Davy asked.

"Ray's in the hospital. It's not good."

Davy's heart stuttered. *Oh no.* He turned to run out, but before he did, he pleaded with the woman he disliked most in this world. "Please, do the right thing."

She flicked her glance to the floor and swayed from side to side. Davy sighed as he looked at her and hated that the only thing he could think of her as a human being was *what a waste*.

CHAPTER TWENTY

DAVY JUMPED up from his chair when Gavin walked into the room. They'd both held vigil by Ray's hospital bed until Davy had convinced Gavin the next morning that he should go home and change and check on Oliver. It wasn't the right time to discuss what had happened with Carmen.

Ray's cancer was entering its final stage, and Ray probably wouldn't leave the hospital again. The pain had been so great he hadn't been able to get out of bed that morning.

Davy just hoped Carmen had let Gavin see Oliver one last time before she left. Gavin was so broken. He'd fallen apart as soon as Davy had made it to the hospital and wrapped him in his arms.

Something about Gavin's wild expression as he came into the room, Ollie on his hip, gave Davy pause as he moved toward Gavin. Gavin was panicking. "She's gone," he said, voice breaking.

"What?" Davy asked, all the air leaving his body. "But, Oliver?"

"She handed him to me and said she'd made a mistake. She said she was leaving him with me. Me! I don't know anything about taking care of a kid." Davy stopped Gavin, whose voice had gotten louder with every word.

"Gavin, calm down," Davy said as he reached for Oliver, whose chin was trembling as he stared at his yelling brother.

"Calm down?"

"Yes," Davy said soothingly. He took Oliver from Gavin, who let go more out of being weak with exhaustion than from wanting to. "You're scaring the kid."

Gavin took a step back from Davy and ran his hand over his face. Davy freaked out in his head for the second he could allow himself. This was *not* what he'd meant. What a selfish, selfish woman.

Davy pulled Oliver's head to his chest as he settled Ollie in his arms. "Mommy said I stay with you and Gavvy. Where did Mommy go?"

"Shh. Little guy, don't worry. Mommy's fine. She just had to go away for now," Davy said more confidently than he felt. "Gavin," he said. Gavin looked at him with bloodshot eyes. God, Davy wanted to comfort him so badly, but it wasn't time for that yet.

"Boys," Ray said from the bed behind Davy.

Davy turned to him. Ray's eyes were cloudy from the morphine drip. Davy put a hand on Gavin's shoulder and led him to the chair by Ray's bed. He knew putting the task of comforting on Ray's shoulders when he was drifting in and out because of pain meds was a lot to ask, but Davy needed some help here, so at Ray's nod of stoned understanding, Davy placed Oliver on the bed next to Ray with the order to be careful. If there was one order he knew Oliver could follow, that was it.

Davy stalked out of the hospital room and called Sean. As soon as he explained what had happened the previous night and then everything that followed, Sean hung up, saying he'd be there soon. Davy couldn't help thinking it wouldn't be soon enough.

He wasn't good with things like this. His own mother's death had been hard enough, Davy avoiding mourners who remembered Mona when she had ruffled more than a few feathers. But he had a responsibility to Gavin and Oliver. He had to be here, even though his instincts had him mapping out the closest stairwells to hide in, as he'd done when Mona was in the hospital after her stroke.

Davy called his uncle next and explained everything, mostly for a sympathetic ear. Drew offered to come in from Spokane, but Davy insisted he stay. There was nothing to be done. Hell, Davy didn't even know what Gavin was thinking yet.

Davy ended the call with his uncle and leaned on the wall outside Ray's room, taking deep breaths. A roiling feeling Davy associated with a panic attack started trying to wrap its suffocating fingers around his throat. *Not now. I can't.* He was so angry at himself. He hadn't had that feeling in so long. This was definitely not the fucking time.

He slid to a squat on the floor and took deep breaths. He filled his lungs with sterile, foul-smelling hospital air as though it was fresh mountain air. The cold from the air conditioning tickled his skin, something to focus on. And focus he did. Bright, fluorescent lighting, chilly air, and disinfectant all anchored him. *You can do this. For Gavin, you can do this.* He felt the moment that the panic receded and smiled to himself.

"Davy?" A voice sounded down the hall.

As Davy stood, hearing a herd of footsteps, Sean, Devon, and Mason all rushed toward him. God, was he happy to see all of them. And Davy had *never* been happy to see a group of men running toward him.

"Davy, how's Gav?" That was Mason. They all started asking questions in unison.

"Guys, hush. Quiet it down." Davy shushed them all. "Thanks for coming." He definitely meant that.

"I told them what's going down," Sean said.

"Well, I doubt they'll let all of you in there, but I know Ray and Oliver will be happy to see you," Davy assured them. "But Gav, he's a wreck and I need to get him by himself for a minute."

"Sure thing. We can handle baby duty," Mason said.

"We can?" Devon asked. Everyone stared at him for a minute.

"Anyway," Sean drawled. "Let's go get our boy. You take him somewhere, we'll handle the rest."

Davy let out a breath and was shocked when Devon pulled him into a clumsy hug. "It's all good, dude."

"Okay, you can let him go now, Dopey." Mason pulled Devon off and Davy could see Devon was sniffling.

Sean rolled his eyes, but patted Devon's shoulder fondly. "There, there."

Davy laughed lightly, and it really helped fend off the last of the panicky feeling from earlier. He was thankful he'd fallen in with this group of friends. He couldn't imagine doing better than these guys.

Sean led the way into the room. "Ray, you old bastard, how do you make hospital white look so sexy?"

Ray laughed, and Gavin looked surprised when all of his friends spilled into the room. Everyone passed out hugs and jokes as though nothing was wrong with being cramped in a hospital room. Davy waited for Sean to signal that they had it from there, and then he grabbed Gavin by the sleeve and dragged him out into the hall. Switching from his sleeve to a strong grip on Gavin's hand, Davy led Gavin to one of the stairwells he'd scoped out.

The door shut behind them, and Davy pulled Gavin down to sit on a step next to him. Gavin looked at Davy, confusion and hurt pouring out of his eyes.

"Oh, Gavin." Davy pulled his lover to him and held him tight. Gavin was so tense in Davy's arms, but he clung to Davy's shirt as if he might disappear. "I'm here, babe. I got you." And Davy did. He had Gavin.

They sat for a long, long time. Gavin had trembled for a while, the gears in his head grinding so loud Davy could hear them. But Gavin never cried. He held it together there in Davy's arms, and Davy just sat silently, letting him do whatever he needed. If he just needed time to think, Davy would let him have it because there was so much to deal with right here and right now.

Eventually Gavin sat up and leaned against the rails of the stairs, looking blankly at Davy. Davy waited him out. He knew Gavin needed to come around in his own time.

"Why?" Gavin asked so quietly Davy would have missed it if he hadn't seen Gavin's mouth move. "Fucking *why*?" Gavin shouted. Davy reached for Gavin, but Gavin flinched away. "Why did she leave *now*?"

Davy looked at his feet. He had to tell the truth. It was now or never. He took a deep breath and said, "It's my fault."

"What?" Gavin's tone was harsh. Davy kept looking at his feet until Gavin grabbed Davy's chin and made him look up. "What did you say?"

"I said it's my fault." Davy wished his voice hadn't shaken so much.

"How so?" Davy could tell Gavin was trying hard to be patient, and under the circumstances Davy understood why it was hard to deal with Davy's inability to just fucking speak.

"I told her to leave, Gavin."

Gavin jumped up, glowering at Davy. "Why in the *fuck* would you do that?"

Davy stood quickly and put his hands on Gavin's shoulders. "She was drinking. A lot."

Gavin deflated. "How do you know?"

"Sean saw her drinking when you guys went to the market." Davy saw Gavin getting worked up again. "He didn't know what to do, Gav. You have to understand. He didn't want to say anything in front of Oliver. Then there was the big family dinner, and he didn't want to spoil that."

Gavin sank back down to sit on the steps, and Davy followed his lead. "Then I went to talk to Ray, but he was already here, which I didn't know when I told her to go away. She was wasted and talking to someone about getting money out of Ray then skipping town after he died. She'd been lying. She was still drinking, and she was never going to stay. So I told her to fuck off. But I didn't know she'd leave Oliver. I just told her not to keep him from you, honest."

Gavin put a finger on Davy's lips to quiet him. "I can't believe you did that."

"I know. I'm so sorry. I shouldn't have butted in."

"No, babe. You don't understand. I can't believe you stood up to her. You just went up to her and told her to go?"

Davy grimaced. "Um, that'd be a polite way of paraphrasing our conversation."

Davy was stunned when Gavin's lips descended on his and Gavin held him close as he delivered a bruising kiss with tongue and teeth and no air. When they separated, Davy felt weak and his mind wasn't functioning properly.

"You, Davy Cooper, are my hero. Don't ever doubt that, okay."

Davy nodded dumbly.

"I'm going to ask you to do something really hard right now, though."

"Anything." That was the truth. Davy knew he'd give Gavin anything he needed.

"I need a little time."

"What do you mean?"

"I mean, I just got my brother kinda dropped in my lap. I have to figure out what that means and I have to do it while preparing for Ray to die. I know this is when they say I'm supposed to hold tighter to those I love, but Davy, I need time."

Davy hated how much his voice shook, but he was so confused when he asked, "Forever?"

"No, Davy. No. Just a little while. I need you, I do. And don't stop coming to see Ray, but while I figure all of this out, I know myself well enough to know there's a fucking major freak-out around the corner, and it seems like every time I freak out, you're the one getting hurt, and I'd like to not do something to make *you* go away forever."

"But, I'd know better, Gavin." Gavin couldn't do this to him. Davy wanted so badly to give him time, but Davy couldn't go back to being alone. He needed Gavin, and damned if he cared how pathetic he sounded. "I need you."

Gavin's eyes were so soft, tears filling them. "I need you too." Gavin kissed Davy so softly. Davy teared up, feeling how close that kiss was to a good-bye kiss. "Davy, you have to think long and hard too. If I really do keep my brother, I'm a package deal with a kid. That scares the fuck out of me, but he's my brother. You made me strong, so I know I can do right by him."

"Gavin, you were always strong."

"Maybe. But you made me better. Never doubt it," Gavin said before kissing both corners of Davy's mouth.

God, Davy hated how much this felt like a good-bye. "What's there to think about?" he asked earnestly.

"Are you ready for that? We're twenty-two, Davy. I don't expect you to be ready for a forever and a kid. We haven't been together that long. I'd rather you go away now if you can't handle it than rush into it and freak out down the road. Oliver can't handle that, and God knows I can't take it. I love you too much already."

Davy knew what his answer was, but something in Gavin's face made him relent. "Okay."

"I'm always here, Davy."

Davy kissed Gavin on the forehead. "Me too, Gav. I love you so much. If you need anything…."

"I'll call." Gavin looked away, chin trembling.

Davy stood and walked out the door, willing himself to follow Gavin's wishes. He didn't have to like it, and he didn't have to stay away for long, just long enough for Gavin to know Davy could keep his word. Even if it hurt like motherfucking hell. This was worse than losing his mother, knowing Gavin and Oliver were live flesh and blood and just miles away but he couldn't touch them.

"Davy?" He heard someone call his name. He couldn't turn around, though. He knew if he did, he wouldn't leave, and Gavin needed space. Davy would give him that.

When Davy stepped into the crowded elevator, he saw Sean standing in the hallway, eyes sad and knowing. The door closed, and Davy's heart shattered.

CHAPTER TWENTY-ONE

DAVY WAS ready to put summer behind him. July was almost rolling to a close and he was grateful. The days were long and so were the lines at the shop. Since an article had been published a few weeks earlier calling Bart's a hidden treasure of the Emerald Coast, business, which was already booming in the tourist season, had tripled. The owner was pleased with the profits, and the employees were over the moon with the overflowing tip jars every shift. Davy couldn't really complain, either. All the work meant he didn't have as much time to obsess on how long it had been since he'd shared his bed with Gavin.

Davy still heard from Gavin if Gavin needed someone to sit with Oliver. Davy loved spending time with the little guy. And Davy still went to see Ray whenever he could. Ray slept more often than not, but that was a relief as most of his waking hours were spent in pain.

Today, though, Davy was exhausted. He'd been with Oliver late into the night while Gavin sat at the hospital after being called in by the doctors who thought it might be Ray's last. Ray had pulled through, and Davy had made it home in time to get a few hours of sleep before another ten-hour day.

Davy was like a zombie as he dropped a scoop of birthday-cake ice cream into a tin for a shake. He was just thinking it'd be a damn hard thing to make it another three hours when the owner wandered behind the counter from the back. That told Davy how tired he was—he'd missed his boss even entering the shop.

"Hey, Davy."

"Oh, hey, Henry." Davy started at the appearance of the man. Henry had been coming in more frequently since business had picked up. He had several businesses around town, so he spread his time evenly among them, but Bart's was his highest grossing at the moment, so he came by to help Davy when he could, and Davy was always happy to see him. They'd become decent friends since they'd had to spend more time around each other lately.

"You look tired. Another late night with the kid?" Henry had gotten about as bad at mothering as Drew. Davy thought they'd be perfect for each other.

"Yeah. A false alarm at the hospital had Gavin out late." Davy had grown accustomed to the sympathetic looks people gave him lately. He supposed he looked like someone who had an impending death in the family. It was hard to shake that kind of sadness. He'd not worn it like a cloak around his mother's death, though. He'd been so angry with her for leaving him to cope with a world he knew nothing about that the mourning fell by the wayside, though he figured that might have been his way of mourning, anger rather than sadness.

"Why don't you cut out early? It's not too crazy in here. I can take it from here."

Davy was too grateful for the offer to argue for propriety's sake. "Are you sure?"

"Definitely. In fact, I'll open up in the morning. You come in at noon instead of nine."

Davy almost collapsed from relief. "Really?"

"Yes. Now go. Off with you." Henry dismissed him, turning to a customer. Davy didn't have to be told twice. He started to clean up from his shift, but Henry insisted one of the night-shift workers could handle it.

Davy stopped by a gyro restaurant on his way home. No way he was cooking. He ordered some carryout that he could scarf down right before passing out. The woman behind the counter told him it'd be twenty minutes before his food was ready, so he collapsed in a sloppy heap on the booth against the wall that was for people waiting for carryout orders. He pulled out his phone to make sure there were no messages that needed his immediate attention.

Nope. No messages was okay with him. That meant no one was dead, no mothers had swooped into town to reclaim their children, and no one needed Davy to come back in to work a few more hours.

Davy looked up on the counter to see if his food had magically finished eighteen minutes faster than he'd been quoted. He caught a familiar form in his peripheral. He turned his head to see who it was and found himself meeting Nate's gaze. Davy withdrew, looking away quickly and twisting his hands in his lap.

"Hey, Davy." *Why, God?* Nate had his hands in the pockets of his chinos. His face wasn't as bitchy as the last time Davy had seen him. In fact, he was looking quite contrite.

"Nate."

"Can I sit?"

"Uh, sure." Davy moved his messenger bag that was taking up the booth seat next to him.

"I love their lamb gyros," Nate said lamely.

Davy had no patience today. "Nate, you don't have to make small talk. You can just sit there. My food won't be much longer."

Nate laughed. "Well, you sure aren't quite so timid these days, huh?"

"What?" Davy's voice was thin from exasperation.

"Okay, so I didn't order anything. I saw you coming in and I decided it was high time you and I had a talk."

Great. "Now's not a good time, Nate. I'm tired."

"Please. I want to apologize."

Well that was…. Davy would *not* look surprised. No way. "Okay."

"I'm sure you figured out by now why I was such an asshole."

Davy frowned and shook his head. No, he actually still just assumed Nate didn't like him or was just a bitchy guy.

Nate sighed. "I was jealous."

Davy snorted. Rich boy jealous of Davy?

169

"I've had a crush on Gavin forever."

"Oh."

"Yeah." Nate looked thoroughly embarrassed. "He wouldn't give me the time of day. He was such a cold motherfucker to me. Of course, that was the appeal. The guy's a badass, or was. The guy everyone wants to tame. Then in waltzes you and you're all shy and I couldn't understand it. I mean, you're cute, but—"

"What's your point?" Davy felt a bit insulted and he didn't like thinking about all the guys chasing Gavin. Everything was still so raw.

"That's why I was rude to you. You're nice. If anyone deserves a chance to be happy with Gavin, it's you."

Color me surprised. "Thanks?"

"I mean it. I'm really sorry. I saw you didn't do well in crowds and I took advantage of it. We don't have to be friends, just know that's not me. I'm not always that person. I'm really sorry."

Davy studied Nate's face for a second. He looked as though he was awaiting a firing range. "It's okay, Nate. I mean, he *is* hot."

Nate let out a surprised laugh.

"And I'm not the kind of guy who holds a grudge, so consider it done, okay?"

Nate nodded, looking at Davy with such relief that Davy couldn't see that mean-spirited Nate he'd known thus far in the man before him.

"Gavin must have really given you hell for you to hunt me down to apologize."

Nate grimaced. "No. I mean, yeah he jumped my ass, but the apology is all me."

"Well, thanks." They fell silent for a moment, and Davy began to wonder where in the hell his food was.

"He misses you, you know," Nate whispered. It sounded like it pained him to say it.

Davy sighed. "I miss him too."

"You're a better man than me. I never would have given him space like you did. I know you well enough to know it's not because you actually had to consider staying there for him and his brother. You're doing it for him."

Davy laughed at how transparent he was. "Yeah. I am."

"Well, you're smart. It's done him good. I've never seen Gavin try so hard to get his shit together. And he's not just doing it for his brother, Davy."

Davy smiled at Nate. "Thanks for saying that. He kept telling me I was the one who needed to think about whether I wanted him *and* a kid, when really it's him who had to figure out if he was going to keep his brother and if he'd have time for me too."

Nate put his hand on Davy's shoulder. "Don't worry. He'll call you soon. I know it. You and Oliver are all he talks about. You've been there in a way he never let any of us be, no matter how hard we tried."

"Order number forty-nine!" the woman at the counter bellowed. Davy looked at his receipt.

"Um, that's me," Davy said, showing Nate the ticket. Nate nodded. "Thanks, for saying… all of that."

"You're welcome. I'll see you around." Nate stood at the same time as Davy. Davy grabbed his food from the cashier with a smile and a thanks. When he turned, Nate was already gone. He hoped Nate knew he really did appreciate the words. After nearly a month apart, it was nice to hear that Gavin still thought of Davy as much as Davy thought of him.

Thanks, Nate.

DAVY HADN'T realized he'd passed out before finishing his food until he woke up wearing his side of rice that he'd started picking at what he thought was only a moment earlier. He groaned miserably because now he'd have to drag his tired ass out of bed and change his shirt.

He looked at his sheets and saw he'd rolled onto the container of hummus he'd had sitting beside him, so now he'd need to change the sheets as well. He stood, ignoring the way his feet complained at holding his weight. He was beginning to wonder when working in a soda shop had become a contact sport, because if he judged by the aches in his body, he was getting tackled at least four times a day.

He wasn't sure what woke him up, but he figured it could be the cold hummus sinking in through his shirt. He almost wished he'd just slept through it, blissfully unaware of how gross it was until he woke, rested enough to take care of the new linens.

He trudged to the kitchen, dumped what was left of his dinner in the trash, and threw his fork into the sink. He pulled off his shirt and tossed it in the open washing machine before going to strip his bed. He just hoped his spare set of sheets was clean. He couldn't remember if they'd made it into the wash on his last laundry day.

When he opened the linen closet, he sent up a prayer of thanks, not even caring that it was silly to be thankful for clean sheets. As he stretched the fitted sheet over his daybed mattress, he heard his phone vibrating. He realized it must be in his bag, and the steady vibrations meant someone was calling. He had a moment of panic as he dug through the messenger bag. He pulled it out just in time for the caller to have given up. He saw it was only seven thirty and he'd received four missed calls, all from the same number.

Janie? He hadn't seen her since he'd last taken her to see Ray a week ago. He couldn't imagine why she was calling. That thought froze him. Well, there was a reason. He hit the Redial button and waited through the ringing until Janie answered with a feeble, sniffling "Hello."

No. His words died in his throat.

"Davy?"

"Uh, yes. Yes, ma'am. What's wrong?"

"Honey, it's Ray."

"No."

He listened as she rustled around, sounding as though she was going into another room. "Sweetheart, I'm at the house with Oliver. Gavin is by himself at the hospital, and he wouldn't let me call anyone for him. But I know he needs someone. He needs you."

"But—"

"No more of his stubbornness. He's been silly for long enough. Please, Davy. Go to him."

Davy nodded, then realized she couldn't see him through the phone. "Okay. I'm leaving now."

"Good," she said quietly. "Good. You bring him home, you hear? His brother needs him."

"Yes, ma'am." Davy hung up after a quick good-bye.

He didn't trust himself for a moment, freaking out briefly. He grieved, hating that he hadn't seen Ray once more before he'd passed, but he figured that was normal. He'd seen the man just two days ago, and he'd seemed so lively. You would have guessed he was going to recover any day now. But didn't they always say you had one last uptick before you went?

Davy took a shuddering breath, then dialed a taxi. After pulling on shoes and a clean shirt, he gathered his wallet and keys. He was surprised when he got downstairs that the taxi driver was already calling to say he'd arrived. He dove in the car and rattled off where he needed to go. He debated calling the guys, but he'd wait until he knew what Gavin wanted to do before he made that decision. He didn't feel it was his to make. He was making a big enough decision rushing to Gavin's side without being summoned. He figured he should only take a little control from Gavin at a time.

When they arrived at the hospital, Davy threw some cash at the driver and didn't even stop himself from running inside. He could feel the tether between him and Gavin pulling him, reeling him in, guiding him home. When the elevator doors opened on the floor Ray's room was on, Davy darted out. When he passed the nurse's station, he nodded to them, receiving waves and sympathetic smiles.

He stopped at the door to Ray's room. He couldn't imagine Ray was still there, but since the nurses hadn't stopped him, he figured that was where he'd find Gavin. He placed his hand on the closed door, looking at the nameplate that no longer said *Raymond Walker*. He closed his eyes, holding off the tears. It wasn't his time to grieve. He had to get Gavin. He had to hold Gavin.

He straightened up, sucked in a breath, and opened the door, then stepped into the room. Gavin sat in the chair, looking at the bed as though he couldn't believe it was empty. Davy didn't know what to say, so he stood silently watching Gavin. Gavin wasn't crying, wasn't showing any emotion at all.

Until he turned his head and saw Davy. It was slow. First his eyes softened, the furrow in his brow smoothing out. Then his lips curled up into a gentle smile, one that broke Davy's fucking heart. Davy took a step forward, holding out his hand. Gavin looked at it for a moment, his smile beginning to quiver. When he flicked his eyes back up to Davy's, they were still soft but brimming with unshed tears.

"Let's go home, Gavin," Davy said quietly.

"Home?" Gavin's voiced rasped.

"Home." Davy smiled.

"Thank God." Gavin literally deflated before Davy's eyes as he stood and moved into Davy's embrace. "Thank God," Gavin said brokenly.

CHAPTER TWENTY-TWO

GAVIN COULDN'T remember any days of his life ever going by in such a blur. He remembered mourning faces and loss so deep that it cut. But he also remembered Davy's calming presence and his friends' love. He'd nearly lost it when he'd said good-bye to Ray and afterward, when Oliver leaned over and kissed Gavin on the cheek before saying so sweetly, "I sorry you sad, Gavvy."

Davy had stayed with Gavin and Oliver the night Ray had died and the night of the funeral, but he'd continued to respect Gavin's request for space in the following days. He'd taken time off work and helped Janie occupy Oliver and make sure Gavin ate one of the dozens of casseroles people had left.

Gavin barely remembered the reading of the will, other than remembering Ray had left his daughter another trust, but everything else to Gavin. His attorney said the permanent residence and substantial money he'd inherited would go a long way with the judge in proving he could provide for Oliver. No one figured it'd be much of a problem, though, since they'd contacted Carmen and she'd agreed she was going to sever her rights to Oliver in favor of Gavin being his brother's guardian. Now he had months of social services visits and a pile of attorney fees to look forward to. Not that it wasn't all worth it. His brother and Davy were the best things he had going for him.

Davy. Davy stood by him, loved him, and had proven he was the stronger of the two of them over and over since Gavin had met him. He didn't feel worthy at all as he looked in while Davy tucked Oliver in for bed. "Davy, you staying tonight?"

"No, little man, I have to go home. But I'll be back in the morning." Davy was so good with the kid. It warmed Gavin from the inside out watching the care Davy took as he tucked Oliver in just the way the kid liked ("snug as a bug in a rug") and kissed him on his forehead.

"Night, Davy."

"Night, Ollie," Davy said as he clicked off the lamp, only the nightlight illuminating a corner of the room. Davy smiled when he saw Gavin in the doorway and held his finger up to his lips as he crept over and closed the door behind him.

Gavin followed Davy into the kitchen, where Davy made sure everything was put away before he picked up his messenger bag. "Okay. Everything is cleaned up. I'll see you tomorrow. Do you need anything before I go? Or when I come back tomorrow?"

Oh, Davy.

"I love you, Davy."

"I love you too, Gavin." Davy put his hand to Gavin's face, and Gavin leaned into the touch and kissed Davy's palm.

"Can I survive this?"

Davy shook his head as though Gavin was being silly. "Of course you can. And you will. For Ollie's sake, if nothing else." Gavin was overwhelmed by Davy's faith. What had he done to earn or deserve that?

"Why did she do this, Davy? I'm afraid I'm gonna screw up everything. She just keeps fucking around with my life."

"Hey, hey." Davy wrapped Gavin up in a hug. When everyone else saw the two of them, they saw Gavin who was nothing but trouble and Davy who was a wallflower, but in Gavin's estimation, if you looked inside you'd see that Gavin was just a scared little boy and Davy was his hero.

"That's the grief talking, Gav. The way I see it, in reality your mom did us all a favor showing up like she did."

Gavin leaned back and looked at Davy as though he was insane. "How do you figure?"

"Well, for me, I see that my mom made mistakes, but she still loved me. I've gotten over all my bitterness because she never abandoned me. If anything she cared too much, but that instilled in me the knowledge, the ability to care for you and for Ollie. Then there's you. She came in and gave you someone who would give you love unconditionally and a chance to prove to yourself that you are good enough, that you're nothing like her." Gavin looked at Davy, mesmerized by Davy's poetic way of viewing the clusterfuck that was the Walker family.

"Davy, I don't know if you're crazy or just—"

"Naïve? So I've been told." Davy laughed, but it was warm and his eyes were full of love. "Gavin, can we be done with this space business?"

Gavin wanted that so much. "I want it to be, but is it that easy?"

Davy chuckled. "Of course it is. I love you, you love me. Ollie loves both of us, and we both love him. We take care of him with the help of all those crazy friends of yours."

"Hey, they're your friends too," Gavin pointed out.

"I refuse to claim them." Davy turned his nose up.

"Davy, are you sure you want *this* for the long haul?"

Davy sobered. "Look, I can't promise forever. Neither of us can. I'd love if it could be. But I can promise I'll love you and that brother of yours until you don't want me to anymore, then I'll probably keep loving you after that because I find I'm kinda stubborn. But I can sure say I hope it's forever. I'm definitely okay with it being a forever kinda thing."

Gavin's heart fluttered. "God, where'd you come from?" He captured Davy's mouth with his and sank into the comfort of coming home there in Davy's arms, Davy's heart, Davy's mouth. They kissed for a long while, holding each other until Gavin could feel Davy's hardness against his own. He pulled his lips from Davy's. "Stay with me, with us. Here."

"Are you asking me to move in?" Davy asked.

"Well, I figure we should do this family thing right. Gotta show the kid the right way to do it." Gavin nipped Davy's lips.

"Um, probably not the best way to put that right now." Davy grimaced.

Gavin swatted him, then took him by the hand and led him down the stairs to Gavin's room. He'd refused to move into any other room yet. He knew he'd have to eventually. He didn't like the idea of the kid trying to come down the dark stairs at night if he needed anything.

When Gavin opened his bedroom door, Davy wrapped around him from behind, kissing his neck. "Damn, Davy. Keep doing that." Gavin's breath sped up and he pushed his ass back into Davy's straining erection. Gavin's own was leaking in his boxers and begging to be released from its prison. Davy reached around and stroked Gavin through his jeans. Gavin let out a moan, then turned in Davy's arms to capture his lips in a steamy kiss, biting into Davy's mouth aggressively. They bucked their hips into each other.

"Out of these clothes," Gavin said as he started pulling at the button on Davy's shorts. Davy did away with both of their shirts. Gavin shoved Davy down onto the bed and with one yank had Davy's shorts and underwear off, revealing all that smooth, honeyed skin and his thick red cock that was leaking a sweet puddle onto Davy's flat belly. Gavin leaned over to lick the precum away, then swirled his tongue around the head of Davy's cock.

Davy reached down, knocking Gavin's beanie off his head so could run his fingers through Gavin's hair. Gavin bobbed his head up and down, just taking in the first couple of inches of Davy's cock, making sure to suck hardest when pulling his lips over the head.

He looked up to Davy, who looked down with parted lips and blazing eyes. Fuck, the boy was sexy as hell. Gavin fisted Davy's cock as he kissed up Davy's body, then came down on Davy's mouth for a salty kiss.

Davy lapped into Gavin's mouth hungrily. "I've missed this so much," Davy said between kisses.

"Me, too, babe." And damn if Gavin didn't mean that. Davy was not only the sweetest fuck Gavin had ever felt, he also never felt as connected to life as he did when he and Davy came together.

Gavin looked into Davy's eyes and almost melted from all the lust and love he saw in those green depths. It was overwhelming, and Gavin's breath hitched for a moment. He was loved. He knew it. Davy was right. He was not his mother. Despite everything, he was loved, and he could love with a depth that ached.

"I want to make love to you."

Davy chuckled huskily. "I thought that's what you were doing. And nice with the corny phrasing."

"Really? You're making fun of me now?" Gavin scowled.

"No. Don't listen to me. Take me, lover."

Gavin smacked Davy's bare ass. "When did you become such a wise-ass, Cooper?"

"I guess it's sexually transmitted, *Walker*." Davy leaned up and kissed Gavin's lips playfully. God, yes. This *was* making love. It was playful and caring.

"I mean I want to *make love to you*."

Davy's chest jerked with the hitching of his breath. "I thought we had that problem—you know—us both being bottoms and all."

Gavin licked Davy's lips. "I said I *usually* bottom."

"Oh" was Davy's breathless reply.

"Can I?" Gavin moved his hand down and traced Davy's hole with a finger. Davy nodded. Gavin kissed him again, not parting their lips as he shoved his own pants and boxers off. Davy opened his legs wider, and Gavin sighed into their kiss contentedly as his hips snugged in as if their bodies were made to fit together. Gavin reveled in the comfort of their kisses as he used his hand to position himself in just a way that he could tease Davy's hole with the head of his cock. He smiled wickedly, enjoying the hiss of pleasure Davy emitted when Gavin nudged the tip against Davy's hole and pushed against it, feeling the muscle give just a little.

"Please, Gav. I want you inside me. I've been dying to feel you inside me."

Gavin's nostrils flared, his entire body heating at the sound of those words. And he couldn't deny the truth of his own need to be buried deep inside Davy's body. Davy: his lover, his best friend.

Gavin reached up to the bedside table. Davy placed a hand on Gavin's chest. "Are you clean?"

Gavin searched Davy's face for a second. "Of course. After you and I were together the first time. Clean."

"Me too. I'm clean as of last month."

"So?"

"Just me and you, Gav. No rubber. That is, if you want."

Gavin had never done it bare, and the thought of doing it with Davy, making that commitment with their bodies, he didn't take it lightly. He knew what Davy was offering, and he felt honored.

"You and me, Davy."

Fuck if the smile that broke out on Davy's face wasn't the most beautiful thing Gavin had ever seen. Gavin found the lube in the drawer in the bedside table and squeezed some on his hand and his cock. He stroked himself once, twice, hissing at how badly he needed to come. When he saw the way Davy sucked on his bottom lip, Gavin almost lost it. He leaned down and kissed Davy hard. Davy returned the kiss with moaning enthusiasm.

Gavin gently pressed his middle finger inside Davy, lubing him. Davy arched his back and opened his mouth in a wide groan. Gavin took advantage, licking around Davy's tongue. He loved the way Davy's mouth tasted.

"Now, Gavin. Please." Davy pushed onto Gavin's finger impatiently. Gavin withdrew his finger and placed his cock at Davy's hole. He looked into Davy's eyes as he breached his entrance. Davy's eyes focused on him intently. Gavin slid in, inch by pleasurable inch, tingling from the heat and tightness of Davy's ass. Davy's muscles massaged him soothingly and they yielded to the taking. Gavin's mouth hung open, a fraction of an inch from Davy, not kissing, just sharing breath as Gavin's balls came to rest against the firm globes of Davy's ass.

"Goddamn, Davy. You're so sexy." Gavin sucked Davy's bottom lip into his mouth. Davy was still looking into his eyes, reaching into his soul.

Gavin's skin was so aware that he was connected to Davy that it made Gavin shudder. It was hard to tell where Gavin ended and Davy began. And Gavin couldn't help thinking that was as it should be.

"Make love to me, Gavin," Davy said with a smirk. Gavin scoffed, but it was lost in Davy's mouth when Davy placed the sweetest fucking kiss on Gavin's lips and squeezed his ass muscles.

"Fuuuuuck." That was the only intelligible thing Gavin could muster as he started moving. Davy's feet locked behind Gavin's back, and his arms wrapped around Gavin's neck. Gavin placed his arms on either side of Davy's head and made love to Davy's mouth with his tongue as his cock made love to Davy's ass.

Davy whimpered as he moved his hips into the coupling, and Gavin's balls started pulling into his body. Gavin felt so impossibly connected to Davy, and he was about to make himself a part of him. "Baby, I'm gonna come."

"Do it, Gavin. Come inside me. I want to feel you lose it." Davy attacked Gavin's mouth again. Gavin pumped in earnest, flesh slapping flesh and the smell of sex making him high. He reached a hand between their bodies and started stroking Davy's cock. It only took a few tugs and Davy's hole clamped tight on Gavin's pistoning cock. Davy threw his head back, exposing his sexy throat as he moaned his completion, spurting his seed over Gavin's hand. Gavin kissed Davy's throat as he gritted his teeth and buried himself as deep as possible, giving in to the white-hot orgasm that tore through his body, dumping his own pleasure deep inside Davy.

They lay together, not wanting to separate for long minutes. Their breathing was heavy and their kisses lazy.

"I told you we'd figure this sex stuff out," Gavin said, waggling his eyebrows.

Davy laughed, looking so full of affection he almost burst from it. He responded in the only way Gavin imagined was appropriate in the situation. He hit Gavin with a pillow.

EPILOGUE

DAVY'S LEG bounced nervously as he looked behind him at the group of people who'd joined them in court. Devon, Sean, and Mason had shown. Nate and his Uncle Drew sat in the bench behind them, both giving a thumbs-up as the bailiff called for the Walkers and Davy Cooper to come to the front of the courtroom.

Davy knew his eyes were probably wide as he held tightly to Oliver's hand and stared at the judge, who studied the paperwork for their case on her desk.

"You okay?" Gavin whispered.

Davy looked at his lover, who held Ollie's other hand, and gave him a nod.

He was nervous, but he was ready for this to be finished. It had taken a year. A year of constant visits from social services and meetings with an attorney that had cost Gavin a lot of money. Davy was shocked at how much social services had dug into. They'd asked about Davy's mom, Gavin's situation. Davy and Gavin both had to attend parenting classes. Since Davy lived with them, he had to go through as thorough a process as Gavin.

Davy had moved in shortly after the funeral. Gavin had taken a job as an art teacher, though he had enough money without the need for a job. The attorney said it'd be best if Gavin had steady employment. Davy continued in his position as GM of Bart's. Henry had even given Davy a raise once he'd finished with his business courses, and offered to extend benefits to Gavin and Oliver if need be. Gavin's job had offered enough benefits for the brothers, though.

Gavin still had days of sadness; he missed Ray a lot. He also went through the occasional meltdown, thinking he was fucking up Oliver and ruining Davy's life. But they got through it. They were strong. They were family.

"So, Walker and Cooper," the judge read off her papers. "We are here in the matter of the minor child Oliver Nathaniel Walker." She flicked her gaze over the three of them. "The biological parents of the minor child have relinquished their parental rights in a previous visit to my court, correct?"

"Yes, ma'am," Gavin's attorney said from Gavin's other side. Carmen had shown up with the necessary papers, but never named the father. He'd signed several affidavits in Maine but wished not to be part of the proceedings. That was fine with Davy. He still remembered some of Gavin's fears of who the paternity may fall to and it was better left as it was in Davy's mind.

"Mr. Walker, Mr. Cooper, you're relatively young to take on so much responsibility, but the mother and children's services both claim you're viable candidates."

"He's my brother. I'm honored to be able to take care of him." Gavin's answer earned a look of respect from the judge.

She turned her intimidating gaze to Davy. He squirmed but said the answer he'd been rehearsing. "They're my family and I love them. I am also honored for the chance to take care of them. Both of them."

The judge smiled. Fucking smiled. Davy felt a bit faint at that approval.

"So this is for adoption of the minor child." Statement, not question. They'd decided Gavin adopting Ollie made the most sense, since Carmen and the father had relinquished rights. It had required more paperwork, but Davy knew it was worth it.

"It says here you'll both be adopting young Mr. Walker, correct?"

Davy snapped his gaze to Gavin. Gavin mouthed, *Surprise?*

Motherfucking surprise of the year. They'd mentioned this once in passing, but Davy had filed it away into his file of *Things Gavin Would Be Uncomfortable Thinking About* along with marriage and wearing a tutu to Pride.

Gavin smiled at Davy, and Davy knew exactly what that meant. This was Gavin saying he had faith in forever too. It had been a long time coming, but he had faith. Davy held his emotions in check as he turned back to the judge, whose eyebrow was quirked. No way she'd missed the original surprise on Davy's face.

"Yes, ma'am," Davy said.

Davy knew the judge couldn't have heard it, but he heard when Gavin let his breath out. "Both of us," Gavin confirmed.

She nodded. "So granted. Oliver, are you okay with that?" She leaned over the bench to look at the youngest Walker brother.

"Hell yes!" Oliver hollered.

The court burst out in a collective groan, Gavin's the loudest. Davy covered his mouth to hide his snigger.

The judge looked at Davy with that quirked eyebrow. "You sure you're up for this? Looks like these Walker men are trouble."

Davy smiled and looked over at Gavin, who was blushing. "Yes, ma'am. Turns out, I love trouble."

KADE BOEHME is a southern boy without the charm, but all the sass. Currently residing in Seattle, he lives off ramen noodles and too much booze.

He is "the epitome of dorkdom," only watching TV when Rachel Maddow or one of his sports teams is on. Most of his free time is spent dancing, arguing politics, or with his nose in a book. He is also a hardcore Britney Spears fangirl and has an addiction to glitter.

It was after writing a short story about boys who loved each other for a less-than-reputable adult website that he found his true calling, and hopefully a bit more class.

He hopes to write about all the romance that he personally finds himself allergic to but that others can fall in love with. He maintains that life is real and the stories should be, as well.

Also from DREAMSPINNER PRESS

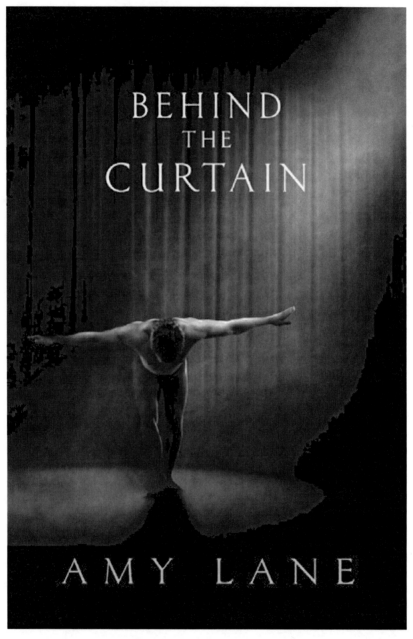

BEHIND
THE
CURTAIN

AMY LANE

Also from DREAMSPINNER PRESS

OUT OF HIDING

MIA KERICK

http://www.dreamspinnerpress.com

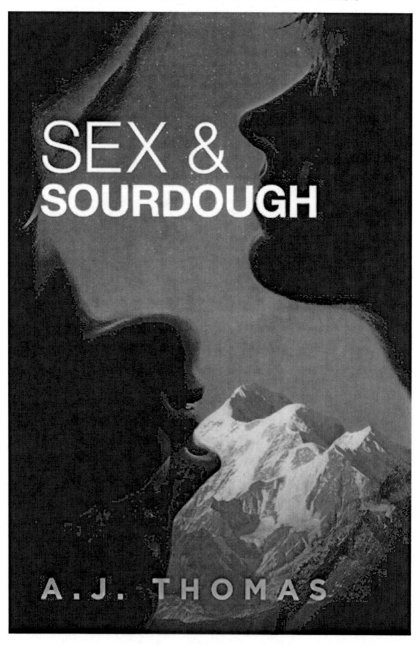

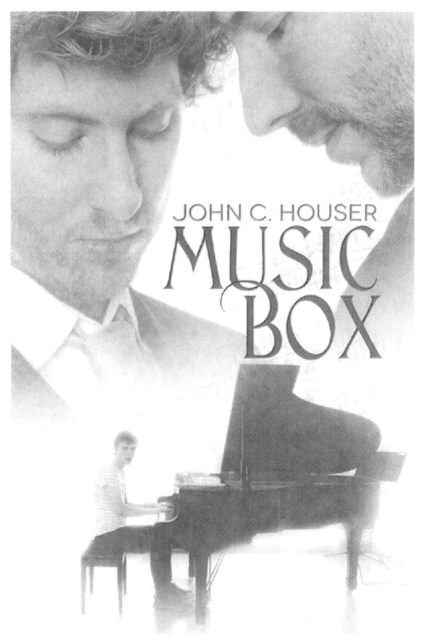

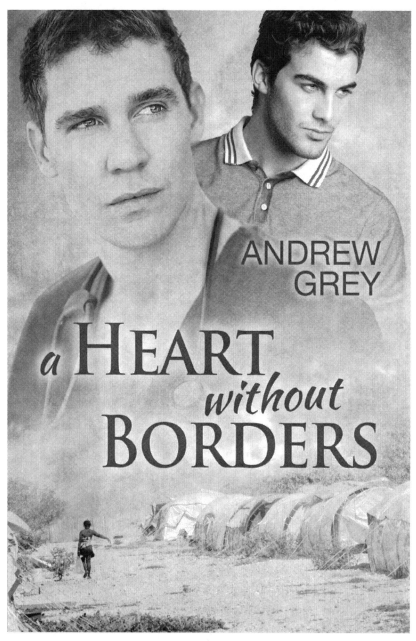

CPSIA information can be obtained at www.ICGtesting.com
Printed in the USA
LVOW09s0243280315

432359LV00004B/16/P

9 781627 984485